THE WEREING

Look for all the books in

THE WEREWOLF CHRONICLES

trilogy:

Book I: *Night Creature*

Book II: *Children of the Wolf*

Book III: *The Wereing*

THE WEREWOLF CHRONICLES

THE WEREING

Book III

Rodman Philbrick and Lynn Harnett

AN
APPLE
PAPERBACK

SCHOLASTIC INC.
New York Toronto London Auckland Sydney

ISBN 0-590-69241-0

12 11 10 9 8 7 6 5 4 3 2 1   6 7 8 9/9 0 1/0

Printed in the U.S.A.   40

First Scholastic printing, September 1996

For Kurt Johnson

RULES OF THE WEREING

1. A werewolf is created by birth or bite.

2. The wereing is the change from human to beast and lasts for the three nights of the full moon.

3. The first wereing of a werewolf child occurs in the twelfth year.

4. If the werewolf child makes a kill in the three nights of the full moon, it shall have all the powers of a full-blooded werewolf and remain a monster forever.

5. A full-blooded werewolf can change into human form at any time, but must become a werewolf when the moon is full.

6. A werewolf cannot cross water.

7. A werewolf cannot tolerate anything silver.

THE WEREING

I am a monster.

For the three nights of the full moon I crouch in the foul swamp outside the peaceful town of Fox Hollow. Seeking the darkness. But there is no escape from the full moon. It turns me into a monster. A hideous, howling beast with thick fur, sharp claws, and dripping fangs.

Each night as the moon rises I am transformed into a werewolf. I prowl through the swamp on all fours, my nostrils filled with the scent of terrified creatures.

It is me they fear.

By day I am a human boy, an ordinary twelve-year-old who goes to school. But for the three nights of the full moon I become a horrible night creature who hungers for blood.

Werewolves bite and kill, that is their nature. But I keep resisting the evil inside me. I have to fight it because —

CRASH! A deer bursts out of the thicket, catches a glimpse of me, and flees in panic. Every fiber of my being yearns to chase that terrified deer. My muscles tense — and then I clamp my powerful jaws shut and force the hunger down, swallowing hard.

1

Yes, I have to fight the monster in me. If I kill just once, I will be a werewolf forever and the people of Fox Hollow will be overrun by the pack of evil creatures who stalk the shadows of night, eyes gleaming like red fire. Werewolves who crave human flesh, especially the blood of children.

I will never be one of them! Never!

The people of Fox Hollow don't know my secret.

Oh, they know that I was raised by wolves — real, magnificent wolves, not the foul creatures of the night.

But if they knew the real truth — that I'd become a werewolf — my new human friends would drive me away, back into the swamp where Wolfmother had found me abandoned as a baby. It was she who raised me with her own cubs, and taught me the ways of the forest. It was she who had tried to protect me from the evil werewolves, and failed.

I could no longer be a wolf. More than anything I want to be human. But whenever the moon waxes full, the wereing begins, and I am a monster again.

I throw back my head and howl in loneliness. "AAAAOOOOOOOOOOOOOOOOOOOOOOOO."

My mournful cry echoes through the swamp,

terrifying the other creatures of the forest. Squirrels cower in the tree branches. Owls screech in panic.

Suddenly a bright light catches my eye. Unlike the silvery cool light of the moon, this light is a golden warmth. The light seems to call, beckoning me to come closer.

I shouldn't go. It is too dangerous — for myself and for the humans of Fox Hollow. But the light fills me with longing.

I run toward the light, unable to resist.

Chapter 2

The wind ruffled my fur as I ran toward the glowing light. My strong lungs filled with sweet, woodsy air. I cleared mossy bogs in a graceful bound and sailed over fallen trees and half-rotten logs. The night was clear as day to my keen eyes and my body sang with the power of the werewolf.

At moments like this I forgot I was a monster. I felt beautiful and wild and free.

Then I reached the edge of the swamp where the trees stopped and the new town of Fox Hollow began. The light glowed softly, drawing me in. But this was as close as I dared to go.

Flicking my tail, I hid among the trees, looking longingly into the light. It was the light from Paul Parker's bedroom. The Parkers were my new human family. They had taken me into their home the day the hunters carried me out of the swamp, away from my wolf family.

These good humans thought I was in my room right now, sleeping. After supper I'd told everybody I didn't feel well and was going to bed early. Mrs. Parker looked concerned. But she thought it was due to the terrifying adventures we'd all had on our school field trip the first night of the full moon.

I hated lying to my new family, but I had no choice.

Paul's window was open to the night air and music from his boom box drifted out to me. I crept closer and watched him squirm and jump around in his chair as he played a computer game. Just like Paul! He was my age and already he was like a brother to me.

As I watched from the darkness, Paul's bedroom door opened and his sister Kim entered. Kim was a year younger. She was pretty good at taking care of herself but I felt protective toward her, just like I had toward the wolf cubs.

There was something about her — I couldn't help it. Maybe it was because the other werewolves, the awful night creatures, seemed to take a special interest in Kim.

I watched Kim and Paul laughing together and wished they could be out here with me. I wished we could all romp together in the woods. Then I shuddered. They'd have to be werewolves to be with me now. That was a fate I wouldn't wish on anybody.

Still, my body tingled with energy. I felt so strong and beautiful I wanted Kim to see how magnificent I was. Surely Kim would see the beauty in me.

My heart thumped with anticipation as Kim started moving slowly toward the window, her eyes sparkling with laughter. I remembered how she made jokes while she taught me to read and speak the human tongue. She never taunted me or made me feel stupid like some of the other kids did.

As she came closer to the window I stepped out of the trees, into a bright patch of moonlight. I could feel how the moon gleamed on my coat and how it made my eyes shine. Any second Kim would see me.

I took a deep breath to swell my great chest.

"Aaaargh!"

What I smelled at that moment brought me to my senses. I leaped back into the shelter of the trees and crouched, sniffing.

The foul stench burned my sensitive nose. It was a monster I smelled — a hideous, revolting werewolf.

And it was lurking in the trees, watching Kim and Paul!

Chapter 3

Anger boiled up inside me as I crept sound-lessly to where the werewolf was hiding. The monster's revolting odor was growing stronger with every careful step. Why was it spying on my friends?

Most likely it wanted to infect them with a bite, turning them into foul creatures like it-self. Or maybe it hungered for their young blood.

Not if I got to it first! My claws itched to sink into the monster's leathery back. Why was it here alone? Were the other werewolves plan-ning something horrible? Maybe this one had been sent to make sure I stayed out of their way.

Baring my fangs, I was determined to get an-swers to all my questions. I crept closer. I could see the werewolf hiding behind a tree and star-ing up at the lighted window, its evil eyes glowing brilliant red. Strings of slobber dripped from its jaws and burned like acid when they hit the ground. The monster was staring so in-tently at my friends it wasn't aware of me.

I knew I would only get one chance. The full-blooded werewolves were bigger and stronger

than me. And I suspected they were more powerful in other ways, too — magical ways I knew
nothing about. If I didn't knock the monster
down the first time, it would get me for sure.

I took a deep breath and leaped.

WHAM!

I landed on nothing but hard ground and dead
leaves. The monster had been too quick for me.
It was gone.

Disgusted with myself I started to brush the
leaves and dirt off my paws. But some bits of it
were stuck. I'd landed on something sticky. I
brought my paw up to my face and sniffed.

Blood! My ears shot up and the hair along my
back stood on end. I dropped to the ground and
sniffed carefully all around. I found a few more
drops, still sticky, as if the werewolf had bitten
something not too long ago.

My blood ran cold. Was I too late? Had the
werewolves already taken over Fox Hollow?
Had they been busy in town while I was roam-
ing the woods?

Tomorrow, I'd know the truth. Exhausted, I
crept behind a tree and slept.

Chapter 4

I woke with the sun streaming into my face. Blinking, I jumped up. I was a boy again! Yes! It was all over — until the next full moon. I grabbed the clothes I had brought out with me last night and pulled them on.

Happy as I was to be human again, I couldn't completely forget that it wasn't really over at all. The other werewolves could change from human to monster any time they wanted. I was the only one who was human all the time except the three nights of the full moon.

But I pushed those thoughts out of my mind and headed for the house. Quietly I unlocked the back door and let myself in. Avoiding the boards that squeaked, I tiptoed to the stairs and up to my room.

A few minutes later Mrs. Parker tapped on my door. "Gruff? Are you awake? Are you feeling any better?"

I opened the door, yawning like I'd just woken up. "I'm fine, Mrs. Parker," I said. "Maybe I just needed some extra sleep."

"That's good," she said, patting my shoulder and smiling happily. It gave me a warm feeling, like she really cared about me. "Why don't you tell Paul to hurry up while I get breakfast on the table."

I knocked on Paul's door and he yelled for me to come in. "Hey, man, you look like your old self again," he said, tugging on a sneaker. "You really looked sick last night."

No, not sick, I thought. Just miserable, knowing I was going to turn into a monster. And hating it that I had to lie to my new family. They were so good to me; but if they knew what I was, they'd all run screaming from me in fear and disgust.

Kim came down late for breakfast, looking sharp in new khaki pants and a bright pink T-shirt. I grinned at her but she just gave me a funny look. Before I could figure out what that was about, Mrs. Parker was talking.

"Kim, did you notice if Dad was up? He's going to be late for work if he doesn't get down here soon," said Mrs. Parker.

Kim shrugged. "I think I heard him," she said. "But I wasn't really paying attention."

We were almost finished with breakfast when Mr. Parker came down.

"You were awfully late last night, dear," said Mrs. Parker. "I must have fallen asleep before you came in."

Mr. Parker looked tired. There were dark circles under his eyes. "Yes," he said, sitting down. "We all had to work late. Some new project they're starting at Wolfe Industries."

Was it my imagination or was Mr. Parker avoiding his wife's questioning gaze? But before I had time to think about it, Paul jumped up. "Come on," he said. "We'll be late for school."

Then as we headed out the door, Kim grabbed my sleeve and pulled me aside. "What's up with you, Gruff?" she asked, searching my face with her keen eyes. "I know you weren't in your room last night."

My heart leaped in panic. Did she know?

"Let's go, you two," yelled Paul from the sidewalk. "We're late!"

"I'm not letting you go till you tell me," said Kim. She was smiling but I could see by the set of her jaw that she meant it.

I swallowed. "Can you keep a secret?"

Chapter 5

"A secret!" said Kim. Her eyes were guarded. "What kind of secret?"

I looked over my shoulder nervously but Kim's parents were talking quietly together in the kitchen. They couldn't hear me.

"I was out hunting werewolves," I said, feeling my heart beat fast.

Kim's eyes opened wide so the whites showed all around. Her jaw dropped. "You didn't go back into the swamp, did you?" she asked in a hushed whisper.

"I had to," I said. "It's not just the swamp, it's the town I'm worried about."

"The town?" Kim shook her head and her shiny brown hair shimmered in the sunlight. "Oh, no, Gruff, those creatures wouldn't dare come near the town. The grown-ups would see them for sure. Right now our parents don't believe in the werewolves. They think we kids panicked that night in the woods. But if they saw those monsters, they'd run them right out of town. As long as we stay out of the swamp we'll be safe," she said as if she was trying to convince herself.

Kim thought the adults were stronger than

werewolves. I couldn't tell her that I suspected some of the adults *were* werewolves. And I didn't believe the adults could save us from the threat of the monsters, anyway. But I couldn't tell Kim that.

"I think the werewolves are plotting to take over the town," I said to Kim. "They're very sneaky. They go after the kids first. You saw that on the field trip. And then, once they've turned us into werewolves, they think we'll bite the grown-ups and infect them, too."

The color drained out of Kim's face. "Gruff, that's horrible," she said. "Horrible!" Her frightened eyes locked into mine. "Then you don't think your wolf family chased the monsters away that night. You think the werewolves will be back to try again, don't you?"

"Yes," I said. "I think they'll be back. But I don't know when."

"What are you two doing?" yelled Paul, scowling from the sidewalk. "Come on, we're going to be late."

Kim shot me one last look full of doubts and worries and questions. Then she ran to catch up with Paul. I followed, a little slower. My feelings were all mixed up. I was glad I had shared my fears with Kim. Now she would be on the lookout for danger — and I believed the monsters wanted her especially, though I didn't know why.

But I felt guilty that I didn't tell her about myself. But how could I tell her? Kim had seen the werewolves. If she knew I was one of those horrible things, she'd run screaming from me. And I might be the only one who could save her. My insides felt queasy just thinking about such a big responsibility.

And here we were walking straight into the biggest danger of all — school. I knew the school was infested with werewolves looking for their chance to turn all the kids into monsters like them. But I didn't know which adults were werewolves and which ones were just ordinary teachers.

But one thing I did know — the werewolves would have their eyes on me. I was like them except that I wouldn't cooperate in their evil plans. And the werewolves didn't let anything stand in their way.

They would be waiting for me. Right insde the school.

Chapter 6

Most of the sixth-grade kids were already in class by the time Paul and I got there.

All the kids seemed nervous, squirming around in their seats and turning pale suddenly for no reason at all.

But it wasn't surprising. This was our first day back in school since the disastrous field trip three days ago on the first night of the wereing.

Our principal, Mr. Clawson, and our gym teacher, Mr. Grunter, had disappeared that night when they took us into the swamp on a field trip. The kids thought the two grown-ups had been caught and eaten by the monsters who attacked our bus. I was the only one who knew that our principal was the leader of the werewolves and Mr. Grunter was a werewolf, too.

"Settle down now, class," said Miss Possum, our sixth-grade teacher. She looked at us sympathetically and smoothed her skirt as she stood up. "I know you're all very upset about Mr. Clawson and Mr. Grunter. But that's no reason to be making up horrible stories. You've frightened the little kids. A lot of parents have called to say the younger children are having nightmares. So, I'd like the rumors to stop right now, do you understand?"

Kids exchanged glances and quickly looked away again.

"Sure, Miss Possum," somebody murmured.

"Okay, Miss Possum," said another.

Miss Possum nodded briskly. "Good," she said. "Now, everyone line up. We're having a special assembly for fifth and sixth graders only. We're going to get this sad business done with, once and for all."

Her lips tightened and her eyes narrowed. My heart lurched. Miss Possum couldn't be one of *them*, could she?

Paul's eyes met mine in a look of alarm. "What's this all about?" he whispered.

"I don't know," I said. My feet felt like they were made of lead as I slowly stood up and got in line. I could see everyone else felt the same way. Some kids were biting their lips so hard they left marks. One girl was tugging on her braid. It must have hurt but she didn't seem to feel it. Her eyes were wide and scared.

What were they going to do to us?

We were the only ones who knew about the monsters. Once they had us all together in one big room they could lock us in. They could force us onto buses and take us on another field trip — deeper into the swamp this time. They'd turn all the kids into werewolves and send them home to infect their parents.

We were doomed, and we couldn't do anything about it!

I opened my mouth to shout a warning. But just then something hit me hard between the shoulder blades, knocking the breath right out of me.

Chapter 7

"Come on, Gruff, move!" urged Paul in a sharp whisper, nudging me again. "Miss Possum's staring at us."

I looked up and met the teacher's eyes. Was she still a human or had she turned into a night creature? I couldn't tell.

I shivered and began moving with the class.

I was glad Paul had brought me to my senses. If I had yelled, it would have accomplished nothing except to scare the other kids and get me barred from assembly. We silently filed down the hall and into the gymnasium. The fifth-grade class was already seated in the bleachers. I waved at Kim but she didn't see me. It was weirdly quiet.

As we sat down I saw Miss Possum closing the big double doors. When she had them secured she leaned back against them, folded her arms, and nodded at someone across the gym. I quickly turned to see who it was.

The fifth-grade teacher stood in front of the emergency exit. He nodded back at Miss Possum, folded his arms, and leaned against the door, blocking the exit. My heart began to pound but no one else seemed to notice we were trapped here.

A lecture stand had been set up and as soon as we were seated, a man came up and stood behind it. He was big and his wiry gray hair was bushy, almost like fur. He held up his hand for silence even though no one was making a sound.

Then he smiled. He had very large teeth. "I am Mr. Smiley, your new principal," he said. "I've called this assembly to tell you that the search party has found no trace of your former principal or your gym teacher. While this is very sad that's no reason to frighten the younger students with ridiculous stories."

Mr. Smiley paused and looked around, frowning so hard his bristling eyebrows met in the middle of his forehead. "We suspect that Mr. Clawson and Mr. Grunter somehow got off the path and slipped into a bog. The bogs in the swamp are very dangerous. Many are full of quicksand and can swallow a grown man in just a few minutes. We may never find their bodies."

Behind me someone whimpered.

Mr. Smiley narrowed his eyes at the sound. "Our search party did find something, though.

What we discovered was" — he paused and looked around to make sure he had our attention. "Wolves!"

"But the wolves helped us!" Kim called out, standing up. "They saved us."

Mr. Smiley turned his terrible gaze on her. "Wolves are vicious, savage animals," he said in a low rumbling voice. "It was the wolves who attacked you, you foolish child."

Kim dropped back into her seat, white and shaking.

"It was clear from their tracks that a pack of wolves attacked the bus you kids were hiding in the night of the field trip. The wolves were obviously in a killing frenzy. You are all lucky to be alive. It seems clear that your principal and gym teacher were savagely attacked by this possibly rabid pack. In their struggles to escape the two men stumbled into a bog — which would explain why we found only a few shreds of their clothing."

Mr. Smiley sighed deeply. "Yes," he said to himself, "that's most likely what happened. But you have nothing more to fear. We will hunt down those murdering wolves and exterminate every last one of them! Now, I want you to go back to your classes and put this behind you. IS THAT CLEAR?"

Under the force of Mr. Smiley's thundering voice, a lot of kids mumbled promises not to speak of monsters anymore. The new principal smiled, showing lots of big yellow teeth. "And now I'll explain some of the new rules that are going to be in force around here," he said. But as he started to talk about hall passes and late notes and detention, my mind wandered.

I was worried about my wolf family. If Mr. Smiley had his way, the humans would be hunting them again. Blaming the real wolves for all the damage the werewolves were doing. But what could I do? How could I convince Fox Hollow about the real danger?

Suddenly, something grabbed my leg.

I squawked and jerked my foot. The thing held on, its claws sinking into my ankle.

It had uncanny strength and it was pulling me down. Down into the darkness under the bleachers.

Chapter 8

I felt myself slipping down and grabbed the edge of the bench, hanging on with all my strength. The principal was still droning on about new rules. No one had noticed what was happening to me but I was afraid to call out.

"Gruff!" somebody whispered.

It was Paul. He grabbed hold of my arm and tried to pull me back into my seat. But whatever had me from below wouldn't let go.

"Wolf-boy!" came a whispered hiss from the dark space below. The voice sounded strangely familiar.

I peered into the darkness below the bleachers. A face appeared out of the shadows. "It's me! Rick!"

Big Rick, the bully, and my enemy since the first day of school. He gave my ankle another tug and let go. "I have to talk to you," he whispered urgently. "Paul, too."

With one eye on the principal I crept down under the bleachers. Paul followed.

"What's up, Rick?" Paul asked. "Why all the secrecy?"

Rick had had close contact with a werewolf and it seemed to have affected him a lot. His face was pale and drawn and I noticed a streak of his hair had turned completely white. A werewolf had pulled him out of a sucking bog, saving his life. Of course, he didn't know the werewolf was me.

"I saw one of those monsters last night," Rick explained, his voice shaking. "A werewolf with gleaming red eyes. It looked about ten feet tall and hairy all over. Horrible! But that's not the worst thing." He shuddered, too overwhelmed to speak.

"What?" asked Paul urgently. "What could be worse?"

Rick started to speak. "It" — his voice cracked. He swallowed and tried again, his terrified voice a raspy croak. "It was prowling around your house."

Paul sucked in his breath. "Our house!"

Rick nodded. "I hid in some bushes across the street. It sniffed around for a while and then I think it disappeared into the woods behind your house. For hours I was afraid to move. I thought it would find me but it was too concentrated on your house. Wow, man, I'd watch out if I were you. There's a monster hanging around right outside your door!"

I tried to look as shocked and horrified as Paul. It wasn't that hard. I really did feel horrible. Rick was right, he had seen a werewolf. But the hideous beast was probably me!

Chapter 9

After the assembly the school settled uneasily back into routine. As the days passed the other kids seemed to slowly forget what had happened and began joking around in class again and meeting after school to play baseball and soccer. In a couple of weeks it almost seemed like nothing had ever happened. For everybody else life was ordinary again.

But not for me. Even though my English was getting so good the other kids no longer teased me about how I talked, I couldn't just relax and be like everybody else. I knew the werewolves would be back. I knew they were plotting something new for the next full moon. I had to do something to save the town and my new family. But what? I wished I knew more about werewolves. Even though I was one myself, I didn't know much about them.

Then I remembered Kim was always going to the school library when she needed information about anything. Maybe there would be something in the library that could help me. I could hardly wait for school to end.

As soon as class let out, I hurried to the library. The door was open but there was no one at the librarian's desk.

"Hello?" I called out.

No answer. There didn't seem to be anyone around. The round tables at the front of the room were all empty. I hesitantly approached the stacks of bookshelves that were arranged in long rows over most of the big room.

My footsteps echoed loudly on the polished wooden floor. There was an itchy feeling between my shoulder blades, as if someone was watching me. But there was no one here. Had to be my imagination.

It was probably just as well the librarian was out, I thought uneasily. I didn't want to explain why I was looking for books on werewolves. But I didn't have any idea where to start looking.

I entered the first row of stacks. The bookshelves towered over my head. I had the oddest feeling that the books on the top shelf were inching forward, about to topple onto my head. But of course when I looked up, nothing had moved an inch.

I tried to shake off my jitters and concentrate. My eye was caught by books on lots of interesting subjects — dinosaurs, spaceships, mountains — but I pulled myself away. For some reason I felt I should hurry, like I didn't have much time.

Reaching the end of the first stack, I turned up the second row. But as I began examining the shelves of books, I heard a board creak. It was coming from the row I had just left! I stiffened and held my breath and listened carefully.

CRRREEEAAK!

There it was again! Someone was stalking me! I hunched over and tiptoed down the row back the way I had come. When I reached the end of the stack, I paused. Then I whipped around the corner and leaped out.

"Gotcha!" I cried.

To the empty air. There was nothing there. The row was empty. I felt really foolish. Wincing to myself, I went back to my search, ignoring the creepy feeling between my shoulder blades. But the itch kept distracting me. It felt like something was perched in a corner of the ceiling, watching me and cackling to itself. But I refused even to look around. It was too silly.

I didn't find any books on werewolves or any kind of monsters in the second stack or the third or the fourth. I was almost halfway

27

through the library. Doors slammed in the distance as the last of the teachers went home. I realized the building must be deserted except for me.

I needed to hurry, or risk being locked in here for the night.

I turned into the fifth stack. Instantly my eyes went to a book that was sticking out at the far end of the row, on the top shelf above my head.

A red-eyed monster stared at me from the cover, as if daring me to come closer. It had a long, evil tongue and sharp, slavering fangs, just like a real werewolf.

For a second I couldn't move a muscle. Then my heart began to pound. The monster on the book cover seemed to grin, as if daring me to reach for it. I was afraid but I was also convinced that there was important information in that book. I had to have it.

My hand was trembling. I reached up. The book was just out of my grasp. I stretched up on my toes as tall as I could but I still couldn't quite reach it. I'd have to climb up on the bookshelves themselves.

The shelves were crowded and I could barely fit the toe of my sneaker on the edge. But all I needed was a few more inches. A quick boost up should do it. I put my weight on my toe and jumped up, reaching for the book with the monster on the cover. I grasped it with my fingertips.

At that instant, the lights went out!

Chapter 10

The room plunged into darkness. I yelped and fell backward. Above me books shifted and began to fall.

CRASH.

"Ow! Ooh!"

Sharp-cornered books rained down on my skull. I scrambled to get out from under. *Something* didn't want me to have that book. But spooked as I was, I hadn't let go of it. I clenched my fingers tighter and pulled the book out of the pile. Then I scurried on all fours to the end of the row.

I heard shuffling footsteps. Something large, headed my way! I had to get out of here. I got up as quietly as I could and tried to remember where the door was. The sound of heavy breathing was confusing my thoughts.

Panicking, I started to run.

"Oooof!"

I ran smack into the corner of a bookshelf, banging my knee. I rubbed my knee, trying not to groan. Which way was the door? Tucking the book under my arm, I inched forward in the darkness, feeling my way, trying to stay absolutely silent.

Was that laughter I heard? Low, evil laughter? Or was it just my blood pounding through my heart?

I kept moving, feeling in front of me with my free hand, fighting the urge to break into a run. Behind me there was a sudden loud clatter. More books falling. I jumped and stubbed my toe on something metal. It skittered across the floor with a shrieking noise.

A chair! Ignoring my throbbing toe I reached out. My hand touched the back of another chair and then the surface of the table. I felt a surge of hope. I'd reached the front of the room where the tables and chairs were arranged. I only had a few more feet to go.

But as I made a dash for the door it swung open. A flood of light blinded me.

"Well!"

I blinked. Standing in the doorway was a small gray-haired lady with her hair twisted up in a bun. She had a ferocious scowl on her face.

"I thought I heard someone banging around in here," she said. "Whatever are you doing?"

I stammered. "I — I wanted a book. Then the lights went out."

"I turned them out," said the lady. "I didn't think anyone was in here. It's late, you know."

I edged toward the door, afraid to look over

my shoulder. "Yes, well, I got my book. Maybe we should leave now."

"Not on your life, young man. Gruff, isn't it?" She frowned and her sharp brown eyes seemed to bore right through me.

My breath caught in my chest. She wasn't going to let me go! It was her all along! And now I was trapped.

She took a step toward me.

I took a step backward.

"I heard a mess of books falling off the shelves," she said. "And you're planning to leave them there for someone else to pick up? I don't think so. We'll just go back there right now and take care of it." She smiled. "I'm the librarian. Mrs. Bookbinder. Come along."

I let my breath out. Maybe she wasn't one of the werewolves. But that meant there was still a monster waiting silently somewhere in the stacks. We wouldn't see it until it pounced on us.

"What are you waiting for, young man?" asked Mrs. Bookbinder with an exasperated sigh. "Let's go. You can show me the books you knocked over."

"Yes, Mrs. Bookbinder." I followed her, dragging my feet. They were itching to run out the door.

"What's the book that was so important?" asked Mrs. Bookbinder.

I didn't want to show it to her but she insisted, prying it out of my hand. "Butterfly collecting?" asked Mrs. Bookbinder, sounding surprised. "How interesting."

What? I looked down at the book I was clutching. "Oh, no," I said. "I picked up the wrong one!"

"No problem," said Mrs. Bookbinder cheerfully. "My goodness, what a mess," she added, looking at the pile of books that had fallen. "No doubt we'll find your book here. What was it about?"

I mumbled something and hurried ahead of her to start picking up books.

"What's that?" Mrs. Bookbinder pushed a wheeled ladder toward me from the end of the aisle. I'd never even noticed it. She got up on the ladder and started shelving books. "I didn't hear you," she said. "What are you looking for?"

"Werewolves," I whispered. My eyes darted over the books on the floor. But I didn't see the cover I was looking for. "I want to know about werewolves."

She jumped down off the ladder and I ducked away, expecting her to turn into a red-eyed monster. She leaned toward me, showing small, pointy teeth.

"No!" I cried, stumbling backward.

Mrs. Bookbinder looked startled. "Are you all right?" she asked, straightening up with a book in her hand.

"Fine," I mumbled sheepishly. "I guess I got a little spooked in the dark before."

"Mmm." The librarian didn't look like she quite believed me. "Is this the book you're looking for?"

She held up the book. I looked at it uneasily. The cover was the same, but different somehow. The eyes were red but they weren't glowing, and the red was too tame. The werewolf's face looked like a cross between a dog and a human. And not a very ferocious dog at that. Even the teeth were wrong. It wasn't in the least scary, now that I had a good look at it.

"Yes," I said, taking it. "I think so."

The librarian chuckled. Then suddenly her face got very serious. "There's something you should know, Gruff," she said, "about that book."

That's when the door slammed open and a voice like evil thunder shook the room.

Chapter 11

"MRS. BOOKBINDER!"

I shuddered in fear as the booming voice rattled the glass in the windows, but the librarian just sighed. "Yes, Mr. Smiley," she called out. "I'm here."

Then she turned to me with a furtive motion. "Quick, Gruff. Take this one, too." She thrust the butterfly book into my hands. "You don't want the principal to see you with a book on werewolves."

Mrs. Bookbinder hurried past me out of the stacks. "I was just helping one of our young pupils," she explained. "Come along, Gruff. Time for you to be getting home."

Pressing the books together so only the butterfly cover showed, I followed her. Our new principal stood in the doorway. There was no room to get by him. "You must be the wolfboy," he said ominously. "I've heard about you."

He stared at me for another long moment. His eyes burned right through me. Then he stepped aside.

I was out of there like a shot!

In spite of my shaking knees, I ran all the way home.

Kim and Paul were doing their homework. Mr. Parker was still at Wolfe Industries and Mrs. Parker wasn't home from her job at the day-care center yet. I hurried upstairs, went into my room, and closed the door.

I tossed the butterfly book aside. But when I finally sat alone with the werewolf book in my hands, I was afraid to open it.

I could see it wasn't a real werewolf on the cover — I knew what *they* looked like! But the book was old and covered in leather. The leather was soft and felt like skin. Not human skin, it was too thick. No, it felt like werewolf skin.

"Go ahead!" I silently urged myself. "Do it!"

Finally I forced myself to open the book. The paper was yellow and crackly.

I still wasn't a good reader even though I could speak almost as good as the other kids now. I'd only been reading for a short time and Kim told me she started learning to read when she was six, so I didn't know if I'd ever catch up. But I figured even Kim and Paul would have a tough time with this book. The printing was small and faded with age. There were a lot of big words, words I'd never heard of.

But I hungered to know what I was. So I began at the beginning. And there, on the first page, were words that struck me with awe and dread.

"RULES OF THE WEREING"

There were seven rules.

Puzzling out the words, I whispered them over to myself, each one like a stab in the heart. When I was done I felt as if the "Rules of The Wereing" had been branded into my soul with hot metal.

The next chapter explained what the rules meant. The book said that "whether born or bitten" a werewolf would not undergo its first wereing — its first change under the full moon from human to beast — until the age of twelve. On its first wereing, the young werewolf had all the qualities of human and beast. However, once the new werewolf made its first kill, it gained the powers of the mature werewolf but it lost its "essential humanity."

The words struck terror into me although I wasn't sure what they meant. Struggling, I read further. The blooded werewolf, said the book, kept the cunning intelligence of its human side but lost its human compassion, sympathy, and understanding of right and wrong. The blooded werewolf was ruled by its thirst for power and its hunger for blood.

The monster's senses — smell, sight, and hearing — were more acute than any wild animal's. Its physical strength was equally supernatural. It could run as fast as the wind, climb the tallest skyscraper with ease, jump as high as a tree.

And the blooded werewolf could transform itself from human shape to werewolf at any time — except for the three nights of the full moon. While the full moon was in the sky, all werewolves were compelled to abandon human form.

The blooded werewolf, the book went on, was intelligent and more powerful than any beast known. Its awesome abilities were equalled only by its evil nature. The werewolf lived only to prey on all living creatures, especially children, and to make more of its own kind.

A chill settled over me as cold as the grave. I'd known I was a monster — now I knew what it meant!

As for the last two rules — that a werewolf cannot cross water and cannot tolerate silver —

they didn't need explaining but they didn't mean anything to me.

After my hands stopped shaking I leafed through the book. There was some stuff about the history of werewolves. The original monsters came from some country I'd never heard of — Transylvania — but no one knew how they got there. Some said it was a curse, some said there had always been werewolves.

As I sat on my bed, thinking about what I had read, numb with dread and worry, my mouth suddenly began to water and my stomach rumbled dangerously. My nose tingled with anticipation.

I sat bolt upright, gripping the edge of the bed. It was the hunger of the beast!

But the full moon was over. What was happening to me?

Chapter 12

"Groooowl." My stomach demanded meat. Had I done something by accident that made me a blooded werewolf?

"Paul, Gruff, Kim! Dinner," called Mrs. Parker.

Dinner! I jumped up from the bed in relief. I hadn't eaten anything since lunch, so of course I was hungry — just like any human. I flung open my door and followed the wonderful aroma downstairs. As usual, I was the first one at the table.

But for some reason when Mrs. Parker dished out the hamburgers and salad, I found I couldn't eat much. I kept thinking of the werewolves' horrible taste for fresh meat.

"Are you all right, Gruff?" Mrs. Parker asked, eyeing my plate. "You're not feeling ill again, are you?"

"Oh, no," I insisted and picked up my hamburger. But I really couldn't take another bite. "It's just that — I was thinking of becoming a vegetarian!"

Mrs. Parker looked startled.

Kim giggled. "Is this the same Gruff who

didn't want to wait for Dad to cook the steaks on the barbecue?" she said, reminding me of a mealtime experience I would just as soon forget. There were a lot of those when I first came to the Parkers'.

"Hush, Kim," said Mrs. Parker. "If Gruff wants to try being a vegetarian, that's just fine." She handed me the salad bowl. "It does mean you'll have to eat your vegetables though, Gruff."

Feeling like a rabbit, which was better than feeling like a monster, I piled more greens on my plate and began munching my way through them.

"That was delicious, Carol," said Mr. Parker. "But now I've got to be getting back." He pushed aside his plate and stood, knotting his tie and grabbing his suit jacket from the back of his chair.

"You're working again tonight?" asked Mrs. Parker, surprised.

"Yes, didn't I tell you?" Mr. Parker glanced at his watch.

Mrs. Parker shook her head but her husband didn't notice. It seemed to me he was avoiding his wife's eyes, just as he had at breakfast that morning.

"Wolfe Industries has started work on a special project," he said. "We're all working nights for a while." He started for the door.

"What kind of project, Dad?" asked Paul.

"Can't talk about it, son," said Mr. Parker, already headed out the door. "Top secret."

After helping Mrs. Parker with the dishes, I hurried back upstairs to read some more about werewolves. I hadn't yet discovered anything in the book that might help me figure out what the werewolves might be plotting or how I might stop them.

But I'd hardly opened the book when there was a knock on my door. I quick stuck the book under my pillow and grabbed a school book instead. "Come in," I called out.

Kim opened the door. She didn't look happy.

"Kim! What's wrong?"

She sighed and walked over to the window. "Did you notice anything weird about my dad today?" she asked.

"Weird?" I didn't know what to say. Mr. Parker had seemed strange and distant but I didn't want to worry Kim.

"He's been acting funny the last few days," said Kim, frowning. "Paul says I'm crazy. But Dad's different. He doesn't seem to notice us. I was telling him about our new principal and he just walked away, like he didn't even know I was there."

"Maybe he's worried about this big project at work." I was trying to be soothing but even as I spoke, an icy tingle of alarm ran down my backbone. What was this project at Wolfe Industries that took up all of Mr. Parker's time?

"Yeah, maybe it's just work," sighed Kim. She perched on the edge of my bed and watched her pink-sneakered foot bob up and down nervously. "But he's never acted like this before. It gives me the creeps. I don't know how to explain it."

Kim raised her face and I would see the terrible fear in her eyes. She whispered, "It's like he's not my real father."

Chapter 13

Kim's words of fear echoed in my head for days: *It's like he's not my real father.*

What did it mean? I watched Mr. Parker whenever I could. He did seem different. Like his mind was far away. He didn't smile and kid around with us like he used to. And every night he went back to work — eagerly. It was like he'd rather be at work than home with his family.

I wanted to pretend none of this was happening. School was going pretty good and some of Paul's friends were starting to accept me. I was learning to play baseball. I didn't want to think about werewolves.

But Kim looked more anxious every day. And the next full moon was coming. I felt like it was already hanging over my head — and that's why I kept reading the book on werewolves, looking for clues.

One night Mr. Parker rushed off to work instead of going to see the school play that Kim was in. Kim was crushed and I couldn't push the questions away any longer.

Could Wolfe Industries be connected to the werewolves? It was Wolfe Industries that had built the town of Fox Hollow. Almost everyone who lived here was connected to the company in some way. But why build the town here?

It was clear I needed to know more about Wolfe Industries. Maybe it had nothing to do with werewolves but every night was another night closer to the full moon and I still didn't have a clue what the monsters were planning. I needed to know and maybe I'd find out something at the big company.

That night I lay awake while the sounds of the house settled around me. Everyone was asleep. Except me. And Mr. Parker. He hadn't come home from work on that "special project" yet.

Very quietly I opened my door. I was dressed in jeans and sneakers and wore a warm sweatshirt. The house was dark except for the hall light downstairs which had been left burning for Mr. Parker.

I crept down the stairs. A board creaked loudly and I stopped, holding my breath. After a few minutes, when no one got up or called out, I continued down.

Shapes loomed up at me out of the dark. My nerves jumped under my skin and the air felt heavy with menace. I twitched my shoulders, trying to shake off the jitters. If I was ready to jump at every shadow in my own home, how could I go out into the night where werewolves might lurk on any corner?

I crossed the kitchen and let myself out. Instantly my heart started to beat faster. Everything inside me was telling me to go back upstairs and go to bed. What could I do, anyway? But I had to find out what was going on, I had to — for Kim.

But first, there was the yard to check. I slipped from shadow to shadow, alert to any sign that a werewolf was lurking, waiting for its chance to prey on my family. Everything seemed quiet. I prowled the backyard and was starting along the side of the house when I heard a noise.

Startled, I whipped my head around. Leaves rustled, something growled angrily. And before I could duck, a blur sprang for me.

"Yyoooowl!"

A cat. It landed on the lawn in front of me and took off. As I got my breath back, I realized the cat was a good sign. It wouldn't have been nosing around here if there had been any werewolves nearby. I took a deep breath. It was safe to leave my family. But my knees were still shaking a bit as I started toward the street.

Maybe that was why I didn't hear him behind me.

The first I knew of any danger was when that big heavy paw came down on my shoulder.

I let out a yell. "Yiiiiiiiiieeeeee!"

A second huge paw clamped over my mouth, cutting off my scream.

And my air.

I had time for one last thought — there had been a werewolf hanging around and even the cat hadn't sensed it.

Chapter 14

I twisted my neck and ducked my head, trying to get free.

"Sssshhhh!"

I froze and strained my eyes to see over my shoulder.

"Be quiet! Do you want to wake everybody up?"

It wasn't a werewolf's paws that had grabbed me, it was only Paul's clammy hands.

"I heard you get up," said Paul, letting me go. "I'm going with you."

There was steel determination in his voice. But I wasn't going to try and talk him out of it anyway. I was glad to have company. Already I felt less scared, although my heart was still pounding from having been grabbed. "You nearly gave me a heart attack," I complained.

"Sorry," said Paul. "But I didn't know how to get your attention without making noise that might wake up my mom. She'd kill us if she caught us out here." He looked up at the darkened windows as if afraid she might hear even his quietest whisper. "You're going to check out Wolfe Industries, right?"

I nodded. We headed for the street and stuck

close to the shadows, circling away from street-lights.

"I told Kim I thought she was imagining things," said Paul in a quiet voice. "But I was only trying to stop her worrying. She's right, Dad *is* acting weird. And it has something to do with his new job."

"He's a chemist, right?" I asked, my eyes probing the darkness for the slightest movement or a glint from glowing red eyes.

"Yes. But I don't know what he's working on," said Paul. "We only moved to Fox Hollow because Wolfe Industries offered so much more money than his old job. But he was always kind of vague about what the company does. It seemed like he wasn't really sure himself."

We passed through the center of town without seeing anything or anyone and turned to the right, heading toward Fox Hollow Pond. It was so dark the surface of the pond looked like liquid metal, gray and shiny.

"I hope we'll be able to go swimming here in the summer," Paul said wistfully. "I hope all this is over by then."

"Yeah," I said. "I hope so, too."

Circling the pond, we passed a small sandy beach. There was a dock built out a little way into the water and a rowboat was tied to the end of it. We could have a lot of fun here this summer — if we lived that long.

Leaving the pond behind, we started up a steep, thickly wooded hill. Along one whole side of the hill was a fenced-in area with some new half-finished buildings and a lot of construction equipment.

"That's the new recreation area," said Paul. "It looks like it'll be done pretty soon. We'll have fun there this summer."

"Mmm," I said, not really listening. My attention was drawn to the top of the hill where the trees had been cleared away to make room for the complex of buildings that made up Wolfe Industries. Glaring white lights blazed out from the roofs of the buildings like spikes jutting into the sky.

We trudged toward the lights, too tense to talk anymore. But we never made it that far.

Chapter 15

Suddenly a tall fence bristling with barbed wire rose up in front of us. The fence gave off a strange humming noise. It was clear we couldn't get any closer to Wolfe Industries.

"I don't remember this," said Paul, sounding alarmed. "I came to work once with my dad when we first moved here. I'm sure there was no fence then."

"What's that noise?" I asked, noticing that the cotton fuzz on my sweatshirt was standing on end. My stomach started to get fluttery.

"It's electrified," said Paul. "They really don't want anyone getting close. Come on. Let's walk around it, see if there's a way in."

But there was no break in the fence. We came to a big double gate, wide enough for large trucks to pass through, but it was closed and locked with a huge padlock.

"I've never seen a lock that big," breathed Paul.

We stood looking in through the gate. We could hear the dull thump of machinery rumbling from inside. After a while a small door opened in one of the buildings. Paul and I shrank quickly away from the fence, into the darkness.

A man came out. We couldn't see what he was doing but he didn't look sneaky or monsterlike or anything. He looked ordinary. After a minute he went back inside and closed the door again.

We stayed where we were a long time, watching. But nothing else happened. I began to think that maybe it was just an ordinary company, filled with ordinary working humans. Mr. Parker was probably just distracted by the exciting new product he was helping to develop, whatever it was.

I started to feel sleepy. "Paul, maybe we should go. I don't think anything — "

A bloodcurdling howl suddenly drowned out my voice.

"AAAAOOOOOOOOOOOOOOOOOO!"

Chapter 16

Paul stiffened and grabbed my arm. "It's coming from inside!"

As the awful sound died away, another howl started up.

"AAAAIIIIIIIIIIIIEEEEEEEEEEE!"

"It's coming from the other side of the complex!" I exclaimed. My voice came out hoarse. All I wanted to do was get out of there. Fast.

"Come on," urged Paul, pulling me toward the awful noise. "This way."

We ran along the edge of the fence. The hum of the electric wires seemed to vibrate with my fright. It was darker at the back of the complex — so dark, anything might be hiding there.

Paul pointed to the one building that was lit up. "The howls must have come from there," he suggested.

We crept closer. "I wish there was some way to get inside this fence," said Paul.

I shuddered at the idea, but he was right. We'd never find out what was going on from way out here.

"Look!" I said, pointing at a sign on the lit-up building.

" 'Experimental Technologies,' " Paul read. "I wonder what that means?"

"There's something moving inside that building," I said, staring toward the lighted windows, feeling my flesh crawl. The strange movements were horribly familiar. Suddenly I wanted to get Paul away from there.

But Paul was already running along the fence, trying to get a better view into the low, narrow windows.

I caught up with him and we crouched on the ground, straining to see inside. The light flickered as large ugly shapes stretched and turned in front of it.

"AAAAAEEEEEEEEEE!"

"AAAAAAAOOOOOOOOO!"

"EEEEEEEIIIIIII!"

Paul and I clutched at each other as a chorus of howls filled the night. We jumped at a sudden noise in a tree behind us. But it was only a bird, terrified out of its nest. It flew away, squawking.

The horrible howling went on, eating into our brains and numbing our ears. "It's them, isn't it?" whispered Paul, his voice quaking. "The werewolves."

I could only nod in the dark. The savage, gleeful howling called to something deep in-

climbed a — tree," panted Paul, his voice ragged from lack of breath.

"No good," I said grimly, my lungs burning. "Werewolves can jump higher than we can climb. Keep running. Our only hope is to reach town!"

Paul didn't question how I came to know so much about monsters. He just ran. But it was hopeless. Behind us the werewolves had fanned out and were coming at us from several directions at once. We were exhausted. Twigs whipped at our faces and brambles snagged our clothes.

I knew the werewolves could see us and smell us. They could have had us by now but they were toying with us, making a game out of it.

At that moment, I wished it was a full moon night. If I had my werewolf powers I could carry Paul right out of here. I was a match for any of them, when the moon was full.

But tonight I was just a puny human.

Suddenly I had a thought. Words from the werewolf book appeared in my mind clear as day. I didn't know if it would work but running wasn't any use. I had to try my new knowledge — or die trying.

Chapter 18

"Go this way, Paul," I cried, my chest heaving with effort. "We've got to get to the pond! It's our only hope!"

"Huh?" But Paul knew better than to wait for an explanation. We raced through the trees, stumbling over roots and dodging werewolves who howled with evil glee, playing with their prey.

My legs felt like rubber and my lungs were on fire. I began to be afraid we wouldn't make it as far as the pond. Werewolf laughter screamed inside my head.

"Your time has come, Gruff!" The familiar monster voice slithered inside my brain. I recognized it. It was Ripper, the leader of the werewolves, the one who had been our old principal in his human form, Mr. Clawson. The townspeople — the human townspeople — thought he had died in the woods. But he was still alive — and as evil as ever. *"You should have joined us when you had the chance. Hahahaha!"*

But suddenly the gloating tone of his laughter changed. The werewolf leader had realized where Paul and I were headed.

"Get them!" he screamed piercingly. *"Get them NOW!"*

His shriek ripped through me like a barbed spike. I stumbled and almost fell from the pain. "Faster, Paul," I yelled. "Faster!"

All around us werewolves were howling. Closing in on us. Their feet thundered and we felt the ground shake under us. They howled for blood — our blood.

Paul whimpered. He had never heard anything more terrifying.

We had almost reached the pond. I could see the water lapping at the edge of the bank and even make out the skeleton structure of the dock. But the werewolves were gaining. Crashing through the bushes, branches breaking and torn leaves thick as rain in the air, they were right on our heels.

I put on another burst of speed although it seemed impossible. I could no longer feel my legs and the sound of my breath drowned out everything but the spine-tingling howls of the werewolves.

Then we raced out of the trees, onto the shoreline. Sand crunched under my feet. I jumped and landed on the dock. Glancing back I saw a pair of glowing red eyes right over Paul's shoulder. He put on a burst of speed and almost caught up to me.

And then — disaster.

"Ooof!" Paul tripped over a rock and went sprawling, inches from the dock.

The werewolf screamed with glee and leaped high in the air. It couldn't miss. It would land squarely on Paul's back.

"Noooo!" I jumped into the water, grabbed Paul's hand and jerked him into the water with me, even though I knew it was useless. The werewolf only had to reach out and catch us both.

THUMP!

The werewolf landed right where Paul had been a second ago.

"EEEEEEEYARRR!"

The werewolf screamed in pain and anger. It had been so gleeful and overconfident that it had leaped too high, miscalculated, and come down on its ankle. It stumbled in the sand for an instant before it recovered and lunged at us.

But that instant was all we needed. Paul heaved himself out of the water onto the dock, with me pulling him. The werewolf, again an instant too late, raked its claws into the water where we had been.

Paul and I threw ourselves into the boat tied up at the end of the dock.

Steam hissed from the water as the werewolf thrashed to its feet.

I fumbled with the rope. The knot was tight and unfamiliar. Panic bubbled up inside me like fizz in a shaken soda. I couldn't undo it! "Stay calm," I muttered to myself, knowing my shaking hands were only making it worse. But the knot was just too tight. I couldn't budge it.

THUD!

My head jerked up. The werewolf had landed on the dock, hissing.

"HSSSSSSSSS!"

Most of me turned to ice but my hands kept working at the knot. And getting nowhere.

It was too late. We were doomed.

Chapter 19

Tensing its powerful haunches, the monster bared its long yellow fangs and snarled. Slowly it raised its claws. Reflected light from the pond glinted off the deadly curved claws as the werewolf snapped them at us. Its eyes glowed hotter, enjoying the terror on our faces.

It sprang.

Behind me, Paul screamed. "AAAAAA-AAAAAAAAAAAAA!"

I held up the rope, pulling it tight in front of my face. The creature's claws were aimed straight for my eyes. I yanked on the rope that held the boat, trying to pull it loose.

The werewolf hit the rope, almost jerking it out of my hands. Its claws cut through the rope like it was butter. The monster screamed in frustration as the boat shot away from the dock.

"GRRRRRRRRRR!"

With the rope suddenly free in my hands, I fell backward into the bottom of the boat. Paul was yelling in excitement and terror. He grabbed an oar and tried to push the boat out farther. But for some reason, the little boat had stopped dead in the water.

I grabbed the other oar, pulling as hard as I could. But we weren't moving.

"RRRRRAAAAAAAAAAAAAWWWWWWW-WRRRRR!"

Paul yelped and I almost dropped my oar as the monster's head appeared over the side of the boat. Its terrible jaws snapped at us, just missing.

The werewolf was stretched full length on the dock, holding the end of frayed rope that was still attached to our boat.

The boat rocked violently as the werewolf grabbed the side of it with both huge paws, its claws scraping splinters from the wood. Paul fell down but held on to his oar. The werewolf lunged for me and missed, raking the air an inch from my ear.

The werewolf was half into the boat, grunting and snarling with the effort of trying to pull the boat back to the dock without overbalancing and falling into the water. I could see steam rising from its ankles, and black patches where the water had burnt its hide like acid.

Paul was gasping, unable even to scream. The monster lifted its head, flicking its tongue at me like a snake. Its eyes were slits of red fire.

There was a snarling chorus of howling from

shore as the rest of the werewolves gathered. In seconds they would swarm onto the dock and help their companion pull us in.

In a fever of fear, I pulled my oar out of the oarlock. I lifted the oar high in the air. And then banged it down as hard as I could on the werewolf's head.

"AAAAAAAAAAEEEEEEEEEEEEEEEEEEEE-EEEEEEEEE!"

The werewolves on shore howled in a frenzy of rage. The noise was so horrible I knew we had to escape or they would tear us to pieces without bothering to kill us first. The werewolf I had hit lifted its head. Blood bubbled and smoked from a cut on its ugly snout. Its eyes flashed and smoldered as if they would burst into flame any second.

The monster gnashed its fangs and sank its claws into the edge of the boat almost lifting us right out of the water.

SLAM!

I smashed the oar down on its huge paw. It screamed hideously and let go. The boat lurched. I smashed the oar down on its other paw. We might just get away!

The monster screamed and swiped at me, catching the oar. In a flash it snatched it from me. With a shriek of triumph it snapped the thick oar in half like a toothpick.

I pitched backward, landing hard in the bottom of the boat. Pain shot up my backbone. I couldn't move.

The werewolf rose on its hind legs. It flung one half of the oar away and I heard it land way out in the middle of the pond with a soft splash.

Then the monster pointed the jagged half of the oar like a spear. It was aimed right at my heart.

Chapter 20

"No!" screamed Paul.

The werewolf bared its fangs in a grin and threw the spearlike oar with all his strength. It was over. I shut my eyes.

The boat rocked and I heard a loud splash. Then a scream of pain. Not mine.

I opened my eyes, amazed to be alive. Paul was digging his oar into the water as hard as he could and the boat was spinning away from the dock. The broken oar floated nearby. The monster had missed!

The werewolf was jumping up and down in such a tantrum of rage that the dock was splintering under it. The other werewolves on shore howled and screamed with fury, spitting and snarling as they leaped helplessly in the air.

"What now, Gruff? Won't they just swim out and get us?" Paul asked in a shaky voice. The boat was spinning in circles from his efforts with the single oar.

I sat up, rubbing my back. "I got this book on werewolves," I told him. "It said that werewolves can't cross water. And from what I saw of the one who fell in, they can't swim either."

"Yeah," said Paul thoughtfully. "It looked like its legs were burned from the water." He switched to the other side of the boat and rowed from there to change direction. I scrambled up and sat beside him so we could pass the oar back and forth between us and keep the boat sort of stable.

"Uh-oh," said Paul, handing me the oar. We were in the middle of the pond, halfway across and he was looking at the shore.

I looked up. The werewolves were running along the pond's edge, still snarling and spitting.

"Looks like they're planning to meet us on the other side," said Paul.

"Well, there's no rule that says they can't go around water," I said, rowing a couple times then passing the oar back to Paul. "They just can't cross it. We'll just have to make sure we don't go near the shore."

Paul was quiet for a minute. Then he asked, "For how long?"

"Until sunrise," I said, hoping I was right. I figured the werewolves probably didn't need to change back into humans when the sun came up, but they wouldn't want the town to see them — not yet anyway. "They'll change back into humans then and go home."

"Wow," said Paul. "So it's really true? These monsters are human?"

I nodded. I couldn't meet his eyes. Paul was learning some of Fox Hollow's secrets but not — to me — the biggest one. He still didn't know that his new adopted brother was a werewolf, too.

"And Mr. Clawson, our old principal, was he a werewolf?" Paul asked.

"He still is," I said. "He's the leader of the pack."

Paul let out a deep breath. "It's great you know all this, Gruff. We're lucky we have you. How did you find out about them? Did you see the werewolves in the woods?"

My heart lurched — did he suspect? "Yes, in the woods," I said. "But only a few days before your hunters found me. I think the werewolves came with the town, Paul. For some reason it's the town of Fox Hollow they're really interested in."

Paul was quiet again. I had a feeling he was thinking about his father and wondering. Red-eyed monsters continued to shriek and howl all around the pond. They had started fighting among themselves and we heard screams of pain mixed with the savage howls.

After a while the noises blended together and

seemed to fade into the background. The motion of the boat was soothing. . . .

Paul's head dropped onto my shoulder and I woke with a start. "Yikes!"

We were only a few feet from shore. Hundreds of glowing red eyes stared at us hungrily. Masses of werewolves were crouched silently on the bank, tongues hanging out, slobbering with anticipation as they waited for the boat to drift just a little closer. Claws twitched, itching to sink into our flesh.

I grabbed the oar and paddled wildly. The frustrated werewolves erupted in furious howls.

"We fell asleep," said Paul with breathless horror. "How could we do that?"

"We better not do it again," I said, handing him the oar. "We'll have to keep nudging each other."

"Deal," said Paul.

And for a long time we stayed awake, poking each other with the oar as we passed it back and forth. But we'd been through a major ordeal. We were exhausted.

Finally even thoughts of being torn to pieces weren't enough to keep us awake.

We slept — and the boat kept drifting.

Chapter 21

CRUNCH!

We didn't wake until the boat hit the shore, its bottom grinding on the pebbly bank.

"YAAAAAAAAAAAA!"

Paul and I both leaped to our feet in panic, yelling. The boat rocked dangerously. Still half asleep, we fell backward into the boat, knocking our one remaining oar into the water.

Paul dove for it, almost tumbling into the pond. I grabbed him and he pushed off from shore with the oar as I pulled him back into the boat. Shaking, we clutched each other.

"We're still alive," said Paul in a wondering voice. "What happened to the werewolves?"

Safely away from the shore, we looked all around, in every direction. No glowing eyes. No snarling monsters. It was still dark but I noticed the sky getting lighter in the east. "It's almost dawn," I said. "They're gone. We made it."

"Wow! We made it, we really did!" Paul slapped my shoulder. "But I can't believe we fell asleep again." His voice was still shaking. "That was dumb."

"Yeah." I shuddered and we started aiming for shore again. "We'd better try and get home before your mom wakes up. She'll never believe us."

"No, she won't," said Paul dejectedly. We fell silent until the boat nudged the shore. We hopped out and pulled the boat onto the bank. "What are we going to do, Gruff?" asked Paul.

"I don't know. I guess we have to find out more about what they're planning," I said, hurrying back to town.

"We need to find a way inside Wolfe Industries," said Paul, frowning.

"Right now we need to get back before your mom wakes up," I said, breaking into a run.

We ran through town and all the way to the Parker house without seeing anyone at all. We paused outside the back door to catch our breath. Paul looked gray in the rosy morning light. I probably looked just as bad. Unlocking the door we tiptoed through the house and up to our rooms without waking a soul. Paul gave me the high sign as he slipped inside his room.

I sat down heavily on my bed and took off my soaking wet sneakers. I thought about lying down for five minutes but I didn't dare. It was almost time to get ready for school.

I was thinking about all the terrifying things that had happened when I heard a car pull into the driveway.

I peeked out the window and saw Mr. Parker getting out of his car. He looked grim and exhausted and his hair was sticking up all over his head. He looked around furtively to see if anyone was watching him. Then he opened his trunk and took out a bundle of something.

He scowled and suddenly looked up at my window. I pressed myself against the wall. When I looked out again Mr. Parker was by the trash can. He lifted the lid and hurriedly shoved the bundle inside.

What was it and why was he acting so secretive about it? I had to know.

I heard Mr. Parker come inside and trudge heavily up the stairs. When the house was quiet again I pulled on my school clothes and slipped out of my room. From my years of growing up in the woods I knew how to move around without making a sound. I let myself out the back door and crept along the side of the house to the trash can.

When I reached for the lid my hand was shaking. But I had to see what it was Mr. Parker threw away so secretively. I lifted the lid and looked inside. There was nothing but some rags and old magazines.

I breathed a sigh of relief. It was just my imagination making Mr. Parker look suspicious. I started to replace the lid when something about one of the thrown-away rags caught my eye. It looked familiar.

Yes! It was the suit jacket Mr. Parker had worn to work! My heart sinking, I pulled it out. The jacket was all torn apart at the seams and ripped right down the center of the back. I stared at it in horror, then shoved it back into the trash can.

That jacket was ripped apart exactly like my clothes had been when I had undergone the wereing and turned into a werewolf!

Chapter 22

When I let myself back in, Mrs. Parker was in the kitchen. She jumped in surprise. "Ooh! You scared me, Gruff," she said, putting her hand over her heart. "What were you doing?"

"I woke up early and went for a walk," I said, avoiding her eyes. I hated it that I was lying to her. "It's a nice morning."

"Yes," she agreed, sounding distracted.

I wolfed down my cereal and left the table, mumbling something about homework as I headed for the stairs.

Back in my room I was gathering up my schoolbooks when Kim knocked on my door.

"I know you and Paul snuck out last night," she whispered, looking back over her shoulder as she came in. "Paul won't tell me anything. But he looks like he saw a ghost. Or something worse. What happened? And don't say 'nothing' or I'll brain you."

I sighed, not sure how much I should tell her. "We went to Wolfe Industries. We couldn't really get near the place but something weird is definitely happening there," I said. "We heard werewolves. And then some of them chased us."

Kim's eyes were wide. "How did you get away?"

I told her about the boat, figuring she might need to know someday that werewolves can't cross water.

By the time I finished telling her about the red eyes glowing along the edge of the pond, her face was chalk white. For a few minutes she didn't say anything. Then she cleared her throat and asked, "Did you, ah, see my dad?"

I shook my head. "No." I decided not to mention finding the ripped up jacket. No way I could tell Kim her father was a monster — at least not until I was absolutely sure. Maybe someone else was wearing his jacket. Maybe it got ripped up in some other weird way. Maybe —

"Kids!" called Mrs. Parker. "You'll be late for school!"

Kim and I met Paul coming out of his room and all of us headed downstairs. Mr. Parker was waiting by the door, sipping a cup of coffee. He had black circles under his eyes. He forced a smile as Kim and Paul said good-bye and headed out the door. Did he notice that neither of them met his eyes?

" 'Bye, Mr. Parker," I said. But as I started to step through the doorway a heavy hand came down on my shoulder. I winced and jerked away, imagining claws ripping through the thin cloth of my shirt.

"You all right, Gruff?" asked Mr. Parker.

"Sure," I said nervously.

"How are you adjusting to life here in Fox Hollow, living among all us humans?" Mr. Parker's shadowed eyes were boring into me.

My mouth was dry and my heart was beating fast. Did he know I suspected him? "I'm fine, Mr. Parker," I said, avoiding his stare.

"You're sure? You don't find anything, well, strange about living with us?" It seemed like Mr. Parker was probing for something.

"Y-y-yes. Everything is strange," I stammered. "But I'm getting used to it." I wanted to bolt out the door but my feet felt glued in place.

Mr. Parker leaned closer to me and lowered his voice. "Maybe one of these nights we'll do something together. Just you and me," he said. "Know what I mean?"

My throat felt like it was closing. "Yes," I squeaked.

The scary thing was, I knew exactly what he meant. He and I were the same. We were both monsters.

Chapter 23

The school day seemed to go on forever.

Everything my teachers said turned into a drone that made me want to nod off. Paul would kick me when I fell asleep in class and I did the same for him.

Just before the bell finally rang, Paul said, "I guess I can't take these late night adventures. I'm going straight home and take a nap."

"Go ahead," I said. "I've got something to do at the school library."

Tired as I was, I couldn't help thinking how the werewolf book had saved our lives last night. Maybe there was another book that held the secret of what the werewolves were plotting — and how to stop them.

The librarian greeted me from her desk as I entered. "Hello, Gruff," she said cheerily. "Can I help you find something?"

"Uh, no, Mrs. Bookbinder," I said, shifting my feet. "I thought I'd just look around a bit."

She nodded, peering at me suspiciously over her glasses. I edged away and disappeared into the stacks as quick as I could. But I felt like her pebbly little eyes were following me, looking right through the shelves of books.

I started scanning the shelves, looking for titles that had "werewolf" or "monster" in them. But I could feel Mrs. Bookbinder watching me. I kept shrugging my shoulders, as if that would shake off the eery feeling of eyes boring holes in my back.

Was she one of *them*?

She's only a little gray-haired lady, I told myself. She has a nice smile and twinkling brown eyes and she likes to see kids read. What would a sweet lady like Mrs. Bookbinder have to do with werewolves?

I slipped a book on mountain climbing off the shelf and hummed to myself, looking casually over my shoulder to see if Mrs. Bookbinder was watching me.

I got a surprise — the librarian had left her desk. The door to the library was shut. She was gone!

Maybe I could find another werewolf book and get out of there before she returned. I stuck the mountain climbing book back in its place and zipped around to the next stack.

"Yaack!" I squawked, startled.

The gray-haired librarian was standing there in the aisle, waiting for me. "I know what you're afraid of," she said, her eyes glittering strangely.

"You do?" My voice cracked. I almost stumbled backing away from her.

"The moon," she whispered, searching my face. "You're afraid of the full moon."

Her clawlike hand reached out for me.

Chapter 24

My breath stuck in my chest as if a fist had choked off my windpipe.

Mrs. Bookbinder's hand touched my shoulder. There were no claws. Her fingers were just fingers. "That's when the werewolves come out in force," she said, staring into my eyes. "That's when they do their worst."

"Werewolves?" I squeaked. "You know about them?"

Mrs. Bookbinder shuddered. "Fox Hollow is crawling with werewolves," she confided. "I've seen them. Late at night they sneak through the streets to meet in the moonlight and undergo the wereing together. You must have seen them, too, or why would you be looking for books on the monsters?"

Her piercing eyes challenged me to answer her. "I — I'm not sure what you mean," I stammered.

Mrs. Bookbinder frowned and sighed. "Unfortunately we don't have any more books on werewolves in the library. They saw to that. They got rid of them all — except one. The best one. I hid that. And when they were gone, I put it back on the shelf, hoping someone would come along and find it. Somebody young and brave. Somebody who can find a way to save Fox Hollow." She paused, her eyes gleaming behind the thick glasses. "Somebody like you."

Me? I wasn't brave. The only reason I knew about the werewolves was because I was one of them. Did she know my secret? I wanted to run right out of the room but my feet seemed frozen in place.

"Everything you need to know is in that book you found here," she whispered, coming so close that strands of gray hair tickled my nose. "Read it carefully. Especially the 'Rules of The Wereing.' "

I nodded vigorously, unable to speak.

"And remember, the werewolves are everywhere" she hissed, her breath hot on my face. "Turn around and they're watching you from behind a human face."

My heart pounded.

Suddenly there was a noise in the front of the room. Mrs. Bookbinder jumped back from me as if she'd been jerked away like a puppet on a string.

The library door cracked slowly open.

Chapter 25

"Hello?" It was a kid's voice. "Anybody here?"

Mrs. Bookbinder stepped crisply out of the stacks. "Rick, how nice to see you," she said. "And what a surprise. It's not often you visit the library. Especially when school has been out for an hour. What brings you here so late?"

Rick! The school bully. Not that he looked like much of a bully right then. He looked kind of sheepish and embarrassed. He caught sight of me and stepped backward, toward the door. "I remembered I had this book," he said. "I thought I better return it."

Mrs. Bookbinder took the book from his outstretched hand. His other arm was hidden behind his back. "My, my," said Mrs. Bookbinder. "This book isn't due for another week. Now, that really is unlike you, Rick. But maybe you're turning over a new leaf?"

"Uh, yeah, that's right," said Rick. His eyes flicked at me then he ducked his head and edged for the door.

Just then I had an idea. "Hey, Rick," I called. "Wait up."

Big Rick wouldn't have come to the library

just to return a book that wasn't even due. Maybe he'd come for the same reason I had — to find out more about werewolves. Rick knew what it was like to be in the clutches of those monsters. He had good reason to want to stop them — and Paul and I could use all the help we could get.

I caught up with him in the hall. He still kept one arm behind his back. "Rick," I whispered, looking around to make sure we were alone. "Have you seen any more werewolves?"

"Werewolves?" He jerked away from me, narrowing his eyes in that mean way he had. "Are you jabbering about monsters again? Grow up, pig face, there's no such thing as monsters!"

For a second I just stood there, shocked, watching him stalking away from me. Then I knew what happened. Rick must think I was making fun of him, joking about monsters. I had to convince him I was for real. I ran after him and grabbed his shoulder. "Rick — "

He spun around and shoved me. "Get away from me, dog breath, or I'll flatten you good!"

This time I didn't go after him. I'd seen that arm he was hiding. It was bandaged. There was blood seeping through the bandage.

He'd been bitten.

Chapter 26

Rick had been bitten by a werewolf! He was one of them. I hurried home, my spine tingling with fear.

Mrs. Bookbinder was right — the werewolves were everywhere. They were getting to the kids now.

Rick must have been sent to the library by an adult werewolf. Sent to see what I was up to!

Beside me in the street a car slowed. I glanced over and two men were looking at me. They must be werewolves! They were going to drag me into the car and get rid of me! I took off running and was halfway down the street before I realized the car had just stopped at a stop sign and then gone on its way, paying no attention to me.

My poor brain was overreacting, seeing monsters everywhere.

I was so shaken I didn't notice the knot of kids on the next corner until one of them called to me.

"Hey, Gruff, where's Paul?" he asked, waving at me. "He was supposed to meet us."

There were six of them, all boys from our class who got together after school to play baseball. They came up to me and stopped, all of them staring at me.

"Hi, guys," I said. "Paul's gone home. He was tired."

A tall boy, Jim, whispered to his friend Bobby, who grinned. "That's too bad," said Jim. "Now we don't have enough kids to play ball."

"Why don't you play, Gruff?" asked a third kid, Greg. "You get the rules mixed up sometimes but at least you have a good arm."

"Yeah, come on," chimed in the others.

I felt flattered. I'd never been invited without Paul. It gave me a kind of warm feeling inside. Then they started edging around me, hemming me in. Jim looked at Bobby, Bobby glanced at Greg, Greg nodded at Billy and Stewart. They stepped in closer — close enough to grab me.

My pulse started to race. I noticed Jim had a big Band-Aid on his elbow and Greg and Bobby were wearing long sleeves even though it was warm. Could they be werewolves? Secret glances passed between them again. "Come on, Gruff," urged Stewart. "What do you say? Let's go."

"No. I — I have a lot of homework," I said. I spun around but they had me completely surrounded. There was no way out. Could they be werewolves, sent to lure me away from town?

Paul and I had seen too much last night. Now the adult werewolves wanted to get rid of us, me especially!

"Come on, Gruff, don't be such a grind," growled Jim.

"You can do your homework later," said Bobby. "We need you here."

I felt a clawlike hand grab my arm. "No!" I screamed, tearing my arm free. I dove between two of the boys and belted down the street, hearing their startled laughter ring out behind me.

I didn't stop running until I reached home. But already I was wondering if I'd been wrong. Maybe they were just being friendly. I cringed to think how silly I looked running away like that. Unless they really were werewolves. Then it wasn't silly at all.

Feeling totally mixed up, I headed upstairs. I was going to bolt my door and lock the window and take a nap. But when I passed Kim's room I heard a sound that put all thoughts of sleep right out of my head.

A noise that chilled me to the bone.

Chapter 27

I hesitated outside Kim's room. The sounds of sobbing wrenched my heart. "Kim?" I called out quietly and knocked on the door.

There was a pause in the sobbing, then a loud sniffle. "Come in, Gruff," Kim said in a teary voice.

She was sitting on the edge of her bed, on her frilly pink bedspread, her face wet. The sparkles in her eyes were dim.

"What's happened?" I asked, rushing over to her. "What's the matter?"

"It's Dad," she said, tears spilling down her cheeks. "Something's wrong with him!"

Anger and fear surged up inside me. "What did he do this time?" I demanded.

Kim shook her head, making her smooth hair spill over her face. I handed her a tissue from the box beside her. "Some of us kids are trying to get up a soccer league for this summer," she said, hiccupping. "I went to ask him about being a coach. He growled at me to go away. Growled! He was almost snarling like an animal. It was horrible."

"Maybe it's just that he's been so busy at

work," I said hesitantly. "He's probably just tired and irritable."

Kim looked at me wide-eyed, like I'd just failed her, too. "No," she said forcefully. "That's not it. He doesn't listen anymore and he never wants us around. It's like he's someone else, not my dad at all."

Kim burst into tears again. I sat beside her and comforted her as best I could. Kim was so happy and full of energy all the time. I'd never seen her like this. I thought about all the afternoons she'd given up playing with her friends to help me learn reading and arithmetic for school, how she always stood up for me when other kids made fun of the wolf-boy who'd grown up in the woods.

I looked around at the ruffled curtains and the hockey stick propped in the corner, the dolls arranged on a shelf and the baseball mitt under her desk. I had to find a way to help.

But could anyone make her dad the way he used to be? Could anyone defeat the werewolves?

I'd thought of a way to find out, but it was dangerous. So dangerous that thinking of it made my mouth go dry and my palms sweat. If I wanted to stop the werewolves I couldn't wait much longer, no matter how scared I was. The moon was already showing in the afternoon sky. It was growing round.

Every night danger moved nearer.

I shuddered, gazing at the moon. The werewolves were so powerful. They were everywhere.

Waiting, waiting.

Chapter 28

The time had come — I had to do something, even if it put my life in danger.

I told Mrs. Parker I was going to bed early. She hardly heard me, she was so preoccupied. She didn't say much, but I could tell she was almost as worried about Mr. Parker as Kim was.

But I didn't go upstairs. I sneaked out the back door and into the garage. Climbing into the back of Mr. Parker's car, I scrunched down on the floor, getting as far under the seat as I could. I was wearing dark clothes but, still, if he looked in the back, he would see me.

I lay there for a long time. My arm went numb and after a while all I could think about was stretching my legs. Then the car door opened. I closed my eyes tight and held my breath, certain I was about to be discovered.

But Mr. Parker settled into his seat and put on his seat belt. I let my breath out. That was a mistake. Immediately I felt I had to sneeze. The carpet fibers were itching my nose something terrible. I rubbed my nose frantically but the sneeze kept building. I couldn't stop it. My eyes watered and my chest burned.

I pinched my nose and pressed my face into

the floor. But nothing could stop that sneeze. It burst out of me — at the same instant that Mr. Parker turned the key and the engine sprang noisily to life. I was safe. My whole body sagged with relief.

Then Mr. Parker tossed a paper bag onto the backseat. As he pulled out of the driveway, the package slipped off the seat and fell on me. A sneeze was nothing compared to this. My skin crawled with fear. As soon as he turned around to get his bag he would find me.

Desperately I pushed the bag back onto the seat. It felt soft. I peeked into the top of the bag. Clothes! Mr. Parker was taking an extra set of clothes to work. I remembered the ruined jacket in the trash. He wouldn't want to come home in ripped clothes again — clothes torn apart by the wereing.

Shivering, I clenched my jaw to keep my teeth from chattering. I wished I was home in my bed or playing a video game with Paul. I wished I was anywhere but in this car, heading for a place so dangerous I might not come out alive.

In just a few minutes the car slowed, then stopped. A heavy gate clanked. Mr. Parker rolled down his window and said something to whomever was guarding the gate.

"GRRRRRrrrrrrrraaaaaaaaawwwwwww!" the guard growled.

At least that's what it sounded like. Maybe I wasn't hearing too well with my face pushed against the floor. Maybe.

My blood thudded in my ears. I was sure Mr. Parker could hear my pounding heart. He drove through the gate and a minute later he stopped again and shut off the car. Now he would turn around to retrieve his bag and see a boy lying on the floor of his car. What would happen to me then?

His hand came groping over the backseat. It almost landed right on me. Mr. Parker grunted. I felt his weight shift in the seat. He was turning to look!

Without thinking my hand shot up, grabbed the bag and pushed it into his hand. I snatched my hand back and froze. Mr. Parker grunted again and the bag disappeared into the front seat. The car door opened. Mr. Parker got out and slammed the door behind him. I waited until the faint sound of his footsteps completely disappeared.

Cautiously I sat up. The parking lot was surrounded by high electrical fences, like the rest of Wolfe Industries. And I was finally inside.

But the ride over had taken too much out of

me. I'd lost my nerve. I'll just stay in the car, I thought, until Mr. Parker comes back and drives home — somebody else can fight the monsters.

But suddenly the dark night was split with a terrible sound.

"AAAAAAOOOOOOOOOOOOOOOOOOOO!"

The howling got into my blood and turned it to ice water.

Chapter 29

The howling was horrible, but it made me realize I had to keep going — I couldn't quit now. I had to find out what the werewolves were planning.

Rolling into the front seat, I opened the door just enough to crawl out of the car. The parking lot was dark and no one was in sight.

I crouched low and zigzagged toward the building. The werewolf howl was coming from somewhere deep inside. I concentrated on finding a way in. If I let myself think about what might happen after that I'd lose my nerve again.

Reaching the building, I leaned against the wall to get my breath. I hadn't realized how scared I'd gotten just crossing the parking lot. The wall seemed to vibrate from the hum of big machines. Taking a deep breath, I crept along until I came to a steel door. I tried the knob. It wasn't locked!

My knees began to tremble. My brain filled with cobwebs of nightmare creatures waiting on the other side. I pushed the images out of my mind and made myself open the door. It was so dark I couldn't have seen a werewolf if it was right in front of me. I shut the door behind me and stood there, letting my eyes adjust.

I was in a hallway with doors along either side of its length. To my left the hall was completely dark, but a faint patch of light shone to my right. The howling had stopped. The building was eerily quiet — nothing but the dull rumble of machines somewhere.

Heading for the faint light, I noticed the rooms along this hallway seemed to be offices. They all looked identical — new and unused — with a computer on every desk.

As I crept down the corridor the light grew brighter. It was shining from around the next bend in the hall.

My footsteps slowed as my heart began to race. I listened hard, expecting to hear the sound of people working. But only silence rang in my ears. Where were the people?

But when a sound came, it wasn't human.

Claws ticked and scraped along the polished floor as if an animal was running.

It was coming my way. I ducked into an empty office and slipped behind the open door.

The sharp clicking of claws on the floor made a stark picture in my mind. But I didn't dare put my head around the door to see. The sound of heavy panting grew louder then abruptly faded away. The creature had bypassed this section and headed for the lighted area.

I took a deep breath and went back out into the hallway. Like it or not, I had to follow the sound of the scuttling claws. That's the only way I'd discover what the werewolves were planning.

I rounded a corner. This hallway was similar to the others, except that it was brightly lit. Overhead tubes shed glaring light onto the stark white walls and gleaming floor. More light spilled from all the offices and rooms along the hall. Some doors stood open, some were closed.

I couldn't go any further. There was no place to hide. Someone would be sure to see me.

But as I stood peeking around the corner, I realized something strange. I hadn't heard a sound. Not a voice or a person shifting in a chair or anything. The place felt deserted even with all the lights. I dropped to my hands and knees and scurried along the hallway.

When I came to the first office, I glanced in. There were papers tossed around and a cup of coffee stood steaming on the desk. But no one was there.

It was the same with all the offices. I turned

into another corridor and it was the same. Offices lit, doors open, not a soul around. Where was everybody? Rising, I continued down the hall, pressed against the wall, peering into the rooms. Trying to figure out what kind of work went on at Wolfe Industries.

"Ooomph!" I tripped over something soft and squishy. My feet tangled in it and I almost fell.

I looked down. It was a bundle of dark cloth. Cautiously I bent to peer at it. It was a security guard's uniform. It had burst at the seams. There was something sticking to it. I picked it up for a closer look.

There was hair on the torn uniform. Werewolf hair.

Chapter 30

With a cry of disgust, I dropped the torn clothing. A tingle of danger electrified my spine. Had anyone heard me?

I hurried down the hall, deeper into the building. The corridor began to twist and turn at crazy angles. I passed an office and saw more shreds of torn clothing thrown all over the desk and computer.

Then, turning another corner, I slid to a stop in shock. The floor was strewn with shredded clothing. A torn sleeve here, a pant leg there. A suit jacket in three pieces, an exploded shoe. The mess looked like the empty husks of body parts.

I knew what it meant. A whole pack of werewolves had undergone the wereing, changing from human to monster.

Farther on I found a deserted workstation. Over one high-backed stool a guard's neatly pressed uniform was carefully folded. For some reason that gave me the creeps even worse than the rags flung everywhere.

The trail of clothing led me deeper and deeper into the building. The rumble of large machines grew louder.

Then I saw a large puddle of something red on the white floor. Horror washed over me like an icy splash. I edged closer, cold sweat trickling down my neck. Had the werewolves killed some human who resisted them? Or — I stopped short — an intruder like me?

I wanted to run away, but I'd come so far through the twisting hallways that I didn't know the way out. I had no choice — I had to keep going.

As I got closer the red stuff changed. It wasn't blood, it was just a red dress! I was so relieved I almost laughed. The bright red dress was split down the back and left tossed onto the floor.

Suddenly the silence was broken.

Voices! Grunting sounds! And heavy, hurrying footsteps. They were coming my way.

Quickly, I ducked into the nearest room.

It was a laboratory. A machine with glass tubing bubbled on a workbench. The liquid in the tubes was a sickly yellow color. Bottles and jars with weird things in them were stored on shelves. It was all very strange and interesting, but I didn't have time to check it out.

Outside the laboratory there were snuffling noises, as if an animal was laughing. My eyes darted around the lab, searching for a hiding place. I couldn't find a safe spot, and the footsteps were getting closer.

Closer.

They were right outside the door.

I spun around desperate for a place to hide.

My sleeve caught on something. As I tried to get free a whole wire tray of test tubes tottered on the edge of a counter. I tried to catch it. Missed!

CRASH!

Chapter 31

I dropped to the floor.

WHAM! The door burst open. "What was that!" someone shouted.

A vile smell rose from the spilled chemicals, making my eyes water and my throat burn. But no chemicals were strong enough to keep my human scent from the werewolves.

Bits of glass fell from my hair, tinkling on the floor, as I skidded away from the mess. Under a lab table I spotted a cabinet. The door was standing slightly open.

I flung myself at it, scrabbled at the door with my nails. I pryed the door open and squeezed myself inside the cabinet. It was too small for me. It didn't matter. I was doomed anyway as soon as the werewolf caught a whiff of me.

Heavy boots crunched on the broken glass. Boots? Werewolves didn't wear boots.

"I don't see anyone," said a hoarse but familiar voice. A human voice. It was coming from the door to the lab so it didn't belong to big boots.

"Rrrrr." The boots kicked at pieces of glass.

I tried to fit more of me inside the cabinet.

Even curled up with my knees against my forehead, an elbow stuck out and I couldn't close the door. If either of them bent over they couldn't help but see me.

"That tray didn't fall over by itself," said a thick, mean voice. The boots began to walk toward me, stopping right beside the cabinet I was hiding in.

Through a crack in the cabinet door, I spotted the uniformed legs of a security guard. "You know what we have to do if we find an intruder?" The guard gave an evil laugh. "Make it go away. Forever."

"There's no place to hide in here," said the other, familiar voice. It was Mr. Parker. He stepped a little way into the room and I could see him. He was still human but his face looked hard and wooden. "Better search the place anyhow," he continued. "If our secret gets out it'll destroy all our plans."

The guard laughed again. It was more like a growl. "Nothing can stop us," he sneered. "But you better go. I'll take care of this little problem."

"Okay," said Mr. Parker. "They're waiting for me. They don't like it when anyone is late."

Mr. Parker went out and the guard's boots moved away. "Come out, come out wherever you are," he snarled. Things clanked and banged together as he moved stuff clumsily, as if he was more used to paws than hands.

"Come out! Right now! If you don't come out right now something terrible will happen!" he roared. "I'll find you even if I have to change to do it!"

He knocked over a glass jar and growled out of his thick human throat. "I'm getting mad," he muttered, coming into my view.

RIIIIP!

His arm started to bulge. Wiry hairs poked out of the rip starting in his jacket. A rumbling sound came from his chest as he messed around with the equipment. His anger was making him turn into a werewolf. When he did he'd find me for sure. And there was nothing I could do to stop him.

Suddenly he let out a triumphant yell.

"GOTCHA!" he shouted, pouncing on something.

When he stood up he had a large brown rat struggling in his meaty hands. "Miserable rat!" the guard cackled.

A rat! A rat had saved me. At least so far. I felt grateful to the poor quivering creature.

"Ha!" said the guard, lifting the animal up so he could look into its little beady eyes with his

103

big evil eyes. "Think you can wreck our lab, is that it, Mr. Rat? I'll show you how we treat visiting rodents around here!"

Then, as I watched in horror, the guard opened his jaws wide and popped the rat into his mouth.

CRUNCH!

His throat rippled as he swallowed. A small curl of tail twitched at the corner of his lips. He snaked his tongue out, snagged the last inch of tail and slurped it into his mouth. He gulped and smacked his lips. Then he opened his mouth again and out came a long, loud belch.

"Mmmmmmm," he muttered. "Good."

Then he burped again and ambled out of the room.

Chapter 32

My stomach heaved and I crawled out of the cabinet onto the floor. My whole body trembled in violent spasms. I heard moaning.

The moaning was coming from me. Clamping my lips shut, I held onto my stomach until I was sure I wouldn't throw up.

After a while — I couldn't tell how long — I got shakily to my feet. All I wanted to do was get out of this horrible place before they found me. I started shaking again, thinking of that poor rat. I knew they would do the same to me and enjoy it even more.

Wolf-boy, they'd howl, licking their chops, *mmmmmm gooooood!*

On rubbery legs, I started for the door. But which way would lead me back to the parking lot? I turned the way I had come but I couldn't remember all the twists and turns.

All the corridors looked the same — silent and empty and blazing with white light. It was like I was in a maze.

Fear crawled around inside my chest as I realized I was headed deeper and deeper into the huge building. Maybe I should turn around. But I couldn't shake off the feeling that if I turned back I'd find that guard waiting for me, grinning with his bloody teeth.

I slumped against the wall. I'd accomplished nothing and now I couldn't even find my way out. Tears burned my eyes. I brushed them away, angry with myself.

Suddenly I froze. What was that sound?

"GRRRRoooooooooooooooooooooooooowl!"

"Grrrrrrrrrrrrrrrrrrrrrrrrrrr."

"RRRRRRRRRRRRRRRRgggggurrrrr."

I'd found the werewolves!

Behind me that guard was lurking somewhere, lying in wait for intruders. Ahead of me were monsters — a lot of them. Plotting.

Which way should I go?

Chapter 33

I moved forward like a sleepwalker. "They'll scent you!" my brain screamed. "Then they'll eat you like a rat!"

But my feet kept going forward. What had I come here for? Why had I already gone through so much danger if I was just going to run away when my chance came to find out what the creatures were planning for Fox Hollow?

I poked my head around the corner. The hallway was dark. But light spilled from a large room at the end of the hall. The room glowed with soft silvery light, like moonlight. As I stared, a large shape flickered along the wall.

It was the shadow of a werewolf.

I needed to get closer. I couldn't see or hear anything from this far away. There were darkened offices on both sides of the hall near the big room. If I could reach them I could hide inside one of the offices and spy on the werewolves.

Crouching, moving as soundlessly as I knew how, I crept into the little office next door to the werewolves.

My heart banged against my ribs. I waited for

the werewolves to scent me and come hunting. There was no escape.

But nothing happened. At last the fear roaring in my ears began to subside and I could hear again.

Next door the werewolves were growling among themselves. Fragments of words began to appear in my head. That was how werewolf speech worked. The monsters couldn't use human language but one werewolf could understand another, hearing the meaning right inside its skull. It made my brain crawl.

But why didn't they scent me? I peeked around the door. The werewolves — about 12 of them — were gathered around a large table. They all had huge, elegantly padded chairs to sit in. Along the back wall were two wide picture windows looking down over the twinkling lights of Fox Hollow.

And along with the werewolves there were two humans scurrying around, handing out sheets of paper. That's why they didn't notice my scent! There were already humans in the room.

My heart seemed to slip back into its proper place. With other humans around, I might even have a chance to get out of there!

"*All right*," growled a huge werewolf, rising

to stand at the head of the conference table.

Some of the werewolves were drooling horribly as their blood-red eyes followed the movements of the two humans in the room. But they jumped to attention when the big monster brought his clawed fist down on the table.

BANG!

It was the leader of all the werewolves — the beast called Ripper! His thoughts were powerful, echoing inside my head. *"Let's bring this meeting to order. Parker! Give us your report."* Ripper's eyes blazed as he dropped back into his thronelike chair — a bigger, fancier chair than the others.

My eyes widened as a vicious-looking werewolf rose on its hind legs. Could that horrible thing really be nice Mr. Parker?

It was.

"You all have a copy of my report," barked the Parker werewolf, licking its fangs. *"And as you can see"* — he waved a clawed hand at several of the other werewolves — *"the formula works. Now even new werewolves, like myself, can enjoy the advantages of the werewolf physical form on any night without having to make the commitment to full-blooded status. Unfortunately, there seems to be no possibility of making a formula that can transform hu-*

man into werewolf without that special were-wolf bite." Mr. Parker fluttered his claws apologetically.

Ripper scowled. "*That's too bad. But at least there will be plenty of strong new werewolves now so we can work through the night. And as I suspect we'll have to be ready in time for our big surprise, is that right?*" He nodded at another werewolf, and Mr. Parker dropped back into his seat with apparent relief.

The werewolf beside him rose. "*We are a little behind schedule.*" The werewolf cringed as Ripper's eyes blazed at him. "*But we'll be ready,*" he added in a squeak that hurt my head. "*At least the adults don't suspect a thing. Some of the children are jittery but we managed to bite several kids, and the ones we couldn't get to, well, no one believes* them."

"*Uh, about the children.*" Parker sounded hesitant. "*Maybe a couple of them —* "

"*What?*" bellowed Ripper. "*Don't you LIKE being a werewolf, Parker?*"

"*Yes, yes, of course I do,*" whined the Parker creature.

"*Then why shouldn't your children like being werewolves, too?*" Ripper pinned him with his fiery eyes.

Werewolves can't turn pale but it almost

seemed like the blood drained from Mr. Parker's monstrous face.

"And if you like being a werewolf now you'll LOVE it once you've made your first kill," growled Ripper. *"Which you will get to do at the very next full moon. Tomorrow night."*

My heart leaped in hope. Maybe all wasn't lost. Mr. Parker hadn't made his first kill! He was like me! There was still a chance to save him. And what was it he had been going to say about the children? Did he want to spare Kim and Paul? Was there a human part still inside him?

"Enough!" growled Ripper so loud that it hurt inside my head. The excitable murmurs of the other werewolves cut off instantly. Ripper rose up again, towering over them.

"You all know our mission. You know your places and your roles. We will not fail! Tomorrow night as the full moon rises we will turn every human in Fox Hollow into a werewolf — all those we don't want to eat, that is!"

A chorus of cackles erupted but cut off abruptly when Ripper raised his paw. *"One kill you leave to me. And we all know who that is."*

"GRUFF!" shouted the werewolves, making my blood turn to ice and my knees to jelly.

111

But Ripper wasn't finished. *"Remember, all the people of Fox Hollow must be made werewolves. Then WE control the town. After that, we'll march on — to the next town! And the next! And the next! Now, get to work!"*

The other werewolves began howling a chant, leaping onto their chairs, cackling and snarling. *"We want the world and we want it NOW!"* they shrieked.

They hurled themselves onto the table and huddled together. Then all at once they raised their hideous snouts into the air and began to howl at the top of their lungs.

"AAAAAAAAAAAAAAAAAAAAAOOOO-OOOOOOOOOOOOOOO!"

The heart-stopping noise echoed off the walls and the ceiling. It built and built and still the werewolves howled for blood, louder, shriller, higher.

Suddenly the huge panes of glass in the picture window exploded, sending jagged shards flying all over the room.

Chapter 34

Shrieking with glee, the werewolves bounded through the shattered windows and raced off into the night, calling to other werewolves still inside the building. Answering howls erupted from all around the Wolfe Industries complex.

I slumped to the floor, ears ringing, my whole body quivering with horror and disgust. I stayed there, unable to move, as the sound of howling drowned out even my thoughts.

I had to get out of there. I had to follow the werewolves. I had learned that, thanks to Mr. Parker's new formula, there were even more of them than there should be on a night when the moon wasn't full. But I hadn't learned the most important thing: What was the "surprise" Ripper talked about? What were they planning for tomorrow night?

Fresh air ruffled my hair. The broken windows! A way out!

I ran into the deserted conference room. I leaped through the picture window into the parking lot and landed running.

Werewolves were streaming out of the building, howling and leaping. It looked like they were going to trample the electric fence in their monstrous frenzy. But slowly the gate began to swing open.

I ran harder, sprinting after the werewolves. The guard at the gate jumped to get out of their way before he was trampled.

The gate started to swing shut. I couldn't make it before it closed again. I was much too far away. I dropped down, hiding behind a car to catch my breath.

Then the guard at the gate dropped to all fours. His body began to bulge. His clothes split and flew in all directions. He was too excited to stay in human form. He was becoming a werewolf. When the wereing was complete he howled and took off after the others, leaving the gate open.

In a flash I was up, dashing for the gate. Ahead of me werewolves disappeared in the trees, howling with evil glee.

I ran through the gate after them. But they were too fast for my weak human legs. They bounded into the trees and were lost from sight. Some of them leaped the fence into the construction area around the new recreation center. And suddenly all of them were gone.

Gasping with fear and exhaustion, I stumbled blindly through the woods, trying to pick up their trail. But the werewolves had disappeared. I had failed. And tomorrow night was the full moon.

Chapter 35

When I got to school the next morning I went straight to the library without going to class. I had the werewolf book with me, the one that spelled out the "Rules of The Were-ing."

There was something about that library — I felt sure the answers I needed were there.

Mrs. Bookbinder got up from her desk as I came in. She smiled as if she'd been expecting me. "Hello, Gruff," she said, her dark eyes gleaming. "I'll be with you in a moment."

The librarian poked her head out the door and looked up and down the hall. Then, nodding to herself, she locked the door and slipped the key into her pocket.

I gasped in fright. Was she one of them? Was she going to keep me here until it was night and it was too late to help anyone?

"No one must disturb us," whispered Mrs. Bookbinder, gesturing me toward the back of the room. "Stay here. I'll be right back."

She's got to be one of them, I thought. My hands got clammy. I rubbed them on my pants as I looked for a way out. But the library only had one door and the windows were too high to climb out of. A cold shiver traveled down my back to my toes.

"Here we are," said a grim, muffled voice behind me.

I spun around, determined to die fighting. But it was just Mrs. Bookbinder, her voice distorted by the effort of carrying a large, heavy book. "Wait," she said as I took it from her. "I'm not finished yet."

She turned around. Next thing I knew she was hunched over and her shoulders were wriggling. My breath caught in my throat. I looked around for a weapon, gripped the chair I was standing next to. I braced myself for the sight of the werewolf as she turned back.

I let the chair fall with a bang. Mrs. Bookbinder looked surprised. She was still just a small, mild librarian. "You seem awfully jumpy, Gruff," she said. "I know you must be tense but we have a lot of work to do."

She closed the drawer she had been rummaging in and put the stack of papers on the table by the book. "These night creatures are very powerful," she said. "Very strong. There's only one way to beat them."

My heart leaped. I knew I'd been right to come here. "How?"

"You have to out think them."

Chapter 36

I slumped back in my chair. I didn't think I was up to outsmarting a whole pack of supernaturally powerful adult werewolves.

But Mrs. Bookbinder went ahead and laid out some old yellowed newspaper clippings on the table. Then she opened the big book to show me more. As she helped me read the clippings, a story began to come together that filled me with horror.

"This has happened before," Mrs. Bookbinder whispered.

It was true. Years before there had been another town built on the same spot. A town called Pleasantville. Mrs. Bookbinder showed me old newspaper articles saying what a perfect place Pleasantville was going to be when Wereing Incorporated was finished with it. More articles told about the wonderful school and the firehouse and the park and recreation center the Wereing company was building.

"Something happened," Mrs. Bookbinder said. "Something evil."

Before Pleasantville was finished, another kind of article starting showing up in the newspapers. The stories were all short and sounded hysterical and crazy. Reports of babies stolen right out of their cribs in the night. People complaining about strange howling keeping them awake and giving them nightmares.

One article described a strange animal running through the streets of the town under the full moon. Another described people behaving strangely and snarling savagely at each other.

"You should read this article," Mrs. Bookbinder suggested. She handed me a yellowed clipping so old and brittle it almost fell apart in my hands.

In the article a young woman claimed her husband was a werewolf. No one had paid any attention but the very next day the woman vanished into the woods, taking her tiny baby with her.

There was something about the article that really caught my attention. I kept coming back to it, feeling a sad heart-tug every time I read it.

"A few days after the woman and her baby disappeared, police from another town came to Pleasantville," Mrs. Bookbinder told me. "They found the whole town deserted. All the residents of the town had disappeared. Just vanished. No one ever saw them again."

"Never?" I asked.

She shook her head sadly. "Pleasantville became a ghost town and eventually all the new houses fell apart. The remains were bulldozed when they started building Fox Hollow."

"I can't believe it!" I cried. "They've tried this before. Taking over a whole town. I wonder what happened to the people?"

Mrs. Bookbinder bit her lip and looked sadly at the clippings strewn over the table. "I don't know for sure. But I suspect some of them got away and never spoke of the place to a living soul. Others were never heard from again. And some, no doubt, became werewolves."

I sat back in my chair, stunned. It all seemed so hopeless.

Mrs. Bookbinder cleared her throat. "There's more," she said, eyeing me worriedly. "Remember that woman who claimed her husband was a werewolf?

"Yes," I said, feeling an odd tickle of excitement. "She disappeared with her baby."

Mrs. Bookbinder nodded. "That's right. Into the swamp." She paused and gave me a sad smile. "That little baby's name was Gruff."

Chapter 37

When I emerged from the library it was late afternoon. My mind was spinning with all I'd learned. But mostly I was just totally stunned by the news of who I was.

My real mother was a human! I tried to picture her in my mind but couldn't. I had one thing from her, though — my name. I'd always thought Gruff was a name I gave myself, made up from the sound Wolfmother made when she called me. But it wasn't. It really *was* my name.

Walking along, I stopped short. A name wasn't the only thing my mother gave me, I realized. She had given me something much more important. My father was a werewolf but my mother was human. That must be why I had resisted killing and becoming a full-blooded werewolf.

Being a werewolf was thrilling and exciting. When I was a werewolf I knew how weak and puny my human self was. But even when the wereing gripped me, the evil of the other werewolves filled me with fear and horror. It was my human side that showed me the hideous werewolves for what they really were. The half of me that was human wouldn't let me fall under their spell.

As I wandered along, my mind filled with wonder, something tugged at my attention. I tried to shake it off but couldn't. I sighed, looking around to see what it was that was bothering me. It couldn't be werewolves — the day still had several hours to go before the moon would come up.

Suddenly I opened my eyes wide. I stopped. I spun around. The streets were deserted! There wasn't a soul around. Not a car, not another person strolling along, or a kid running to a friend's house — not anyone.

Where had everyone gone? Had they disappeared like the people of Pleasantville? Had the werewolves completed their plan while I was locked in the library?

I tried to remember how long it had been since I'd seen anyone. Had I seen another person since I came out of the library? A hollow panic spread in my chest.

Maybe it was too late.

Suddenly I jerked my head up. What was that strange music? The sound was distant and I knew I'd never heard it before. What could it mean?

Chapter 38

I ran toward the music through the empty streets. "Hello!" I yelled. "Anyone around?" The windows of the houses stared back at me blankly. No curtains twitched, no one curiously stuck a head out a door.

The air was warm but I felt cold.

The music pounded a beat in my head. It was loud and cheerful but it only chilled me more as I got closer. Something big was happening.

Then I rounded a corner and skidded to a stop, staring in amazement. I'd found the townspeople! All of them, it looked like.

A lot of people were in the middle of the street, banging drums and blowing horns, making the odd music I'd been hearing. Other people in the street were dressed in funny clothes and arranged in lines and columns. They were marching in time to the music, lifting their knees up high and grinning at the rest of the townspeople, who were lining the street on both sides, watching them and clapping.

A girl marched in front, wearing a shiny costume and white boots, throwing a metal stick in the air.

"Hi, Gruff!"

It was Kim, wearing her cheerleader outfit, marching with the other cheerleaders, waving pom-poms. She laughed at the expression on my face. "It's a parade," she shouted over the music. "Wolfe Industries is holding a cookout for the whole town to celebrate the opening of the new recreation center. It was a surprise. Didn't you hear the announcement this morning at school?"

I hadn't, of course, because I'd been in the library. All day I'd been studying old clippings while the werewolves were putting the finishing touches on their big "surprise." My heart sank.

Kim waved again as the cheerleaders passed me by. "See you at the rec center," she called back.

My brain felt numb as I watched the columns of Boy Scouts and Girl Scouts go by. Next the town's two policemen glided by in their cruiser. Then a fire truck all decked out in crepe paper streamers.

A murmur went up from the crowd. "Oooooh."

I followed their eyes and saw the strangest thing yet. I had no idea what it could be. It looked like a platform decorated with flowers that spelled out WOLFE INDUSTRIES.

"What a lovely float," said a woman beside me. "Isn't it marvelous?"

I nodded and tried to smile. Everything certainly looked like harmless fun. But I knew it couldn't be.

The first float-thing went by. Little girls stood under make-believe trees. The girls wore ruffled dresses and threw paper flowers at the crowd. People shouted with glee and leaped in the air to catch the red, white, and yellow flowers.

Behind that float came another, even bigger. On this one were two large plastic statues. One was a smiling cow, the other a smiling pig. Standing between them was Mr. Parker!

As I watched, he lifted a megaphone to his lips and shouted, "Come one, come all to Wolfe Industries' cookout. It's a barbecue; it's a carnival; it's fireworks! Come to the party!"

Looking at the grinning plastic animals, I gagged. They were grinning all right. It wasn't beef and pork that would be on the menu at this barbecue — it was Fox Hollow!

Chapter 39

As the last float went by, the people on the sidelines rushed into the street, following the parade to the recreation center grounds on the hill below the Wolfe Industries complex. They streamed by me like a flood.

"Don't go!" I shouted. "You're in danger! They only want to get you all in the same place so they can turn you into monsters like them!"

Some people laughed. Others made a wide circle around me, not wanting to come too close. I heard people whispering about the "strange wolf-boy" who would never learn human ways.

I felt helpless. But somehow I had to stop this. I darted into the crowd and grabbed a woman by the sleeve. She pulled away, gathering her three small children close.

"Listen," I begged. "Please listen. There used to be a town here before Fox Hollow. Strange things started happening just like here and then suddenly all the people disappeared. Wolfe Industries is trying to get everybody together so they can make us all disappear. It's happening again!"

The woman stared at me in disbelief. "It's a

cookout," she said. "Just a simple cookout." The children looked at each other uncertainly but the woman pulled them away and they hurried off, disappearing into the crowd.

I tried again, stopping people and explaining to them what I'd learned that day in the library. They just looked at me as if I were crazy and then ignored me.

I realized I'd never convince the adults. I had to get the kids to help me. I stopped a boy I knew from school. "Marshall, listen to me. You've got to help!"

"Sure, man," he said, snapping his gum. "What's up?"

Everything spilled out, all of it. But halfway through I noticed his eyes straying impatiently to the crowd running into the rec area.

"Look at the size of that Ferris wheel," he interrupted me excitedly. "I hear they have an awesome roller coaster, too. Chill out, Gruff. These guys are just businessmen, trying to show the town a good time." And off he ran.

Nobody would listen! The kids were running to be first on line for rides and the adults were congratulating each other on having moved to such a great little town.

I started looking for Paul. He'd believe me!

The recreation area was spread out below the

big complex of Wolfe Industries, as if the company was watching over it. The rec area — a ball field, playground, rec building, and pool — had a shiny new fence around it. As people waited to get inside the gate I ran along the outside, hunting for a sight of Paul.

Beyond the recreation center was the pond where Paul and I had first escaped the werewolves. But when I came to the pond, I stared in shock. There was nothing left of the pretty little pond but a big mud hole with a little scummy water puddled in the middle.

"Hey, Gruff." I spun around. It was Big Rick, grinning at me.

"Neat, huh," he said, cocking his thumb at the pond. "The guys at Wolfe Industries said it would breed mosquitoes so they drained it. Who cares, anyway? The company built an Olympic-size swimming pool in the rec building. That's better than some muddy old pond. The fire department is filling the pool right now."

I realized that all of this was the "project" the werewolves had been working on. They'd completed it in time and I had never guessed. Did this mean they had won for good?

Rick had taken the bandage off his arm and the scabby marks of werewolf teeth were clearly visible. "You ought to come inside," he said. "You're missing the party. We wouldn't want you to miss the party, would we?"

I raced away from his evil grinning face, ran through the gate, and threaded my way through the crowd.

Where was Paul?

People were chomping on cotton candy and popcorn. A band had set up on a stage and men were firing up huge barbecue grills. There were fire trucks parked by the big rec building.

My brain was working feverishly as I took in every detail of the rec area. There must be something here I could use to convince people. Some mistake the werewolves had made that would show people what they really were.

I passed a woman talking to her daughter. "Sorry, honey, but the man said there won't be any hamburgers ready until after the fireworks," she explained to the girl.

That was it! I'd throw off the lids of those giant coolers and show the people there wasn't any beef waiting to go on the big grills. I'd tell them *they* were going to be on the menu — unless they wanted to be werewolves instead. That should convince them!

But it was hard getting through the crowd. People seemed to knot around me wherever I moved. Big men knocked me off course then grinned into my face, their eyes flecked with red. Sharp-clawed fingers plucked at my clothes, slowing me down. The more I struggled, the more people pushed me backward.

"All right, everybody, get ready," someone shouted from the stage. "It's just about time for the fireworks."

Fireworks! I stared in dismay at the sky. The sun was sinking. The full moon was about to rise!

Chapter 40

It was too late to convince people. I'd have to shout a warning and hope I could scare people into running away.

I took a deep breath. It would have to be the best shout ever. I opened my mouth — and my jaw locked. The only sound that came out of me was an eery mournful howl.

The wereing! The Change was starting. I was about to become a werewolf!

Crouching, I fell back and slipped through the crowd. My arms and legs were tingling with the power of the wereing. I loped for the rec building — already I was faster than the human Gruff. Behind the building, in the quiet darkness, I felt my muscles ripple and grow.

I opened my mouth and sharp fangs shot from my gums while my snout lengthened and filled with all the wonderful smells of the night — denied to me as a human. My eyes glowed and night became bright as day to my sharp eyes.

Dropping to all fours I stretched my powerful back.

RIIIIIP!

My clothing tore at the seams and fell away

from my sleek, muscled limbs. More muscles rippled under the skin as the power of the moon flowed into my legs and arms. My smooth claws shone in the moonlight. Swept up in the thrill of the wereing, I lifted my magnificent head and howled.

"AHHHHOOOOOOO!"

I was Gruff! The beautiful and strong!

As my howl died away I dropped back onto my haunches. I could hear every sound of the crowd — a crying child, laughter, confusion. And under all that the growling of werewolves, getting ready to work their evil.

Instantly I knew myself for what I really was — not beautiful and strong but a hideous and unnatural monster!

Then my keen ears picked up an ominous sound.

CLICK!

The werewolves had locked the front gate. So that's why they'd put up the fence. It was the only exit! The townspeople were trapped.

Chapter 41

BOOOM! CRACK! BOOM!

Everybody was looking up into the sky as colorful fireworks burst overhead.

"Oooooooooh," they cried joyfully. "Ahhhhhhh."

They were so intent on the show they didn't see the werewolves creeping in from the edges of the crowd, red eyes flickering hungrily under the rainbow colors of the fireworks.

A little girl screamed. "Mommy! Look! Monsters!"

The mother looked around, laughing. Then she caught sight of me.

Soon other people were screaming as they glimpsed the glowing eyes and gleaming fangs of the monsters surrounding them. But the explosions of fireworks drowned out their cries.

BOOM! BOOM!

People were running and shoving in panic. They would trample each other once they realized the gate was locked. Already people were falling to the ground and screaming in terror.

I could save them if they'd only listen. I knew what to do. I streaked around the crowd and then leaped into the air, sailing over their heads.

I landed smack in the center of the stage, scattering terrified musicians.

I grabbed the microphone. I can save you, I wanted to tell them. If you'll only listen to me.

I opened my jaws to shout but all that came out was a howl, tremendously magnified by the loudspeakers.

"AAAAAAAAAAAAAAAOOOOOOOOO-OOOOOOOOOOOOO!"

Chapter 42

I gnashed my teeth in frustration. People ran screaming. A werewolf lashed out with its claws and pounced on a fleeing man. There was something oddly familiar about the werewolf.

As the man struggled wildly, the drooling monster sank its teeth into his arm. With a pain like a knife in my heart, I recognized the werewolf. It was Mr. Parker. He lifted his head, fangs dripping, and laughed.

"HEEEEEHAHAHAHHEEE!"

The man dropped to the ground, writhing. Instantly bristly hair began to sprout and the man's clothes ripped at the seams and fell away from his bulging new werewolf body. The man leaped up and began to race after the humans, fangs gleaming wetly.

They were going to do it, I thought. The werewolves were going to take over the town. I saw two of them stir up the fire on the barbecue grills, their eyes glowing hotter than the coals.

Then I caught sight of Paul and Kim. They were running toward the rec building, urging others to follow. My heart gave a leap of hope.

That's right, I shouted inside my head, go to the rec building. It's your only chance!

I jumped off the stage and began hissing and growling, driving the terrified people toward the building.

Werewolves howled in frustration but I lashed at their faces and drove them back. One of the werewolves leaped in the air in front of me. With a little shiver, I recognized Big Rick, the bully from school.

"You can't stop us," he taunted inside my head. *"We're on to your tricks!"*

With a cackle of werewolf laughter he leaped again and opened his paw. From one claw dangled the key to the rec building.

"We'll lock 'em in," he crowed, *"and pick them off one at a time. They'll all join us — whether they want to or not!"*

Chapter 43

The Rick werewolf danced away from me, swinging the key, howling with glee.

Suddenly a pigeon, flushed from its hiding place in the rain gutter of the rec building, burst into flight over Rick's head. The blood urge blazing in his eyes, Rick swiped at the bird and captured it easily.

"No!" I screamed, launching myself into the air.

I crashed into Rick, knocking him to the ground.

"Ugh!" With the wind temporarily knocked out of him, his paw opened and the bird flew off. Rick let out a bellow of anger.

"Don't make your first kill," I growled. *"Or you'll be one of Them forever."*

"Good!" shrieked Rick, struggling. *"I like being a werewolf. What's so bad about it, sissy-monster? I'm strong and powerful, not like those weak humans. Werewolves can do anything!"*

"Werewolves KILL people," I hissed into his ear.

For an instant he went slack. *"No, we just make them werewolves like us,"* he muttered.

But the red glow dimmed uncertainly in his eyes. I hauled him up and dragged him to a toolshed next to the rec building. Yanking open the door, I tossed him inside. *"If you know what's good for you,"* I snarled. *"You'll stay here until dawn."*

I slammed the door and snapped the shed padlock shut. It wouldn't keep him in if he really wanted to get out. I looked at the key I'd taken from him. He could break down the door. And the werewolves could break down the locked rec building door. But if I locked the rec building door it would give the humans a few more minutes.

I ran to the spot where I'd undergone the wereing. Precious seconds ticked by while I searched for my werewolf book. Finally I spied it half buried under a pile of leaves and grabbed it up.

Kim was frantically beckoning stragglers into the building. She didn't see the huge monster coming at her from behind. Ripper, the leader of them all! With a flick of his hairy paw he knocked a burly man head over heels.

"Out of my way," he snarled, although the humans couldn't understand him. *"The girl is mine!"*

I leaped over the heads of a woman and two

children running in panic. But Ripper was faster than me. *"Kim,"* I screamed. *"Look out! Run into the building!"*

But of course she didn't understand. All she heard was the bloodcurling shriek of a monster. Startled, she looked my way. And froze in terror at the sight of a horrible red-eyed monster bearing down on her with what looked like murder in its eyes. Rigidly still at the sight of me, she was a perfect target for Ripper.

With a silent howl of triumph, Ripper sprang, straight at Kim. He grinned at me, fangs dripping, eyes blazing with anticipation. I was too far away to save her.

But out of the dark another werewolf leaped on Ripper. It was Mr. Parker! My heart skipped with joy. He would save Kim!

But Ripper batted the Parker werewolf away with one hand, tumbling him head over heels. Instantly three other werewolves appeared, pinned the Parker werewolf's arms, and dragged him away.

Kim was doomed. Ripper's teeth were set to sink into her shoulder. She was about to become one of Them! With all my strength I leaped, clearing a whole crowd of panicked humans. But Ripper was too close and I was too far away.

Ripper landed on Kim's back, knocking her to the ground. People shrieked and scattered, leaving her to him. Kim's voice was cut off in mid-scream.

RIIIIIP!

My keen ears winced at the sound of her T-shirt tearing as the werewolf sunk his claws into her back.

Chapter 44

Laughing, the werewolf lifted Kim high into the air, his claws curving around her thin arms, his eyes casting a fiery glow on her terrified face. Kim's small fists beat at his hairy face and her sneakered feet kicked as hard as they could.

"HAHAHAHAHAHAHA!"

Ripper laughed, toying with her. His fangs dripped, boiling the dirt under his feet. *"She's mine,"* he gloated as I rushed at him.

Another werewolf leaped out of the shadows and slammed into me, knocking me to the ground.

"Heeeelp!" screamed Kim, kicking with all her might.

Ripper opened his huge jaws, fixing his eyes on Kim. I slashed at the werewolf who had attacked me. It screamed in pain and rage and I kicked it aside. I was too late to save Kim from being bitten but I had to try and get her away from Ripper.

Another werewolf leaped at me. I rolled on the ground and caught the monster on my feet, letting its forward motion help me to throw it into the air. The werewolf crashed into the fence and I bounced to my feet, running.

Just as I ducked to fend off a third werewolf attack, I glimpsed a small dark shape come hurtling out of the rec building doorway, aimed straight for Ripper's head. Ripper was just about to sink his fangs into Kim.

The werewolf's foot connected with my head and for a second I was blind as it wrestled me to the ground and I sunk my teeth deep into its arm. The werewolf screamed and I flung it aside, lunging once again for Ripper.

Ripper's slobbering mouth was wide. He was bellowing with rage and gnashing his huge teeth. The small figure I'd seen was Paul. He had his legs wrapped around the werewolf's massive arm and was poking a stick into the monster's snarling face. Trying to hold a kicking, yelling Kim in his other arm, Ripper couldn't push Paul away.

But I knew it would only be a second before the much bigger, stronger werewolf had the situation under control, with both my friends in his clutches.

I flung another attacking werewolf out of my way and sprang at Ripper.

"YYYYEEEEEEEEEEEEEIIIIIIIII!" I screamed as I landed perfectly, coming down, clawed feet first, on Ripper's head. I sunk my fangs into the arm holding Kim. Ripper's paw spasmed and Kim fell to the ground.

But instead of running she began to pound her little fists against the arm that clutched Paul. "Let go, you horrible monster," she yelled. "Let go of my brother!"

Ripper snarled and struck like a snake to close his fangs on my neck.

At that moment Paul poked his stick right into one of the werewolf's glowing eyes.

"*UUURRRRGGGH!*" Ripper screamed and tossed Paul away as if he were a rag doll.

Kim ran to her dazed brother and I slammed both feet into Ripper's chest, knocking him backward. It was just enough to let me get away. I scooped up Paul and Kim and pushed them — gently — into the recreation building. Quickly I locked the door.

Inside the rec building people fled shrieking at the sight of me. Paul, his eyes wide with terror and rage, rushed at me to save his sister. I grabbed him easily and pulled him aside, wishing desperately that I could talk to humans. But I couldn't.

Throwing down the book, I opened it to the "Rules of The Wereing." Paul stared at me, rigid with fear. Kim pounded on my back, screaming. I snarled and banged my fist on the book. But Paul was afraid to take his eyes off me. I grabbed his head and forced him to look.

With one curved claw, I jabbed at the line I wanted him to read. Paul gasped with understanding. Then he looked at me with questions in his eyes. Did he recognize me? I thought he did.

But there was no time. Already the werewolves were thudding against the rec building door.

CRACK!

The door bulged and began to splinter.

Chapter 45

I gave Paul a gentle shove. He started and tore his eyes away from me.

"Everybody," Paul yelled. "Into the pool. Now!"

CRASH!

A werewolf paw punched through the rec building door and the howling outside built to a frenzy. People whimpered and clutched at one another.

"Come on!" Paul shouted urgently, his voice cracking with strain. "The monsters can't get us in the water. Hurry!"

He started pushing people into the pool with Kim's help. I stayed behind him, waving my long furry arms and growling. A few people got the message and jumped into the pool. Others, trying to escape me, fell in.

"Werewolves hate water!" Paul cried, shoving more people ahead of him. "It burns them. We'll be safe in the water."

Hurrying to get everybody into the water, I stumbled over the thick fire hose that was filling the pool and fell in a slick puddle of water. I skidded toward the pool on my back. Piercing screams hurt my ears as people rushed deeper into the water, thinking I was going to slide right in on top of them.

But I managed to stop myself, just short of the edge. I scrambled to my feet, surprised the water hadn't burned me. But I'd been in water before without being hurt. It must be that my human half protected me.

The door splintered into pieces. Werewolves came pouring in. The air filled with the sound of screams and splashes as the last of the townspeople rushed toward the pool, diving, jumping, and falling into the water.

A window shattered as more werewolves forced their way inside, howling for blood. Then the noise of the monsters changed.

"ARRRRRRRRGGGGGGGHHHH!"

They bellowed in fury, catching sight of all the people huddled in the big swimming pool. Raging, they stomped around the pool, snarling and hissing in frustration.

All at once they fell silent and turned in a mass to face me. The silence was scarier than their horrible screams. They bared their fangs and fixed their glowing red eyes on me as if their glare would burn right through me.

"Come on," I screamed at them inside my head, too shaky to think straight. *"Come and get me you miserable monsters!"*

146

Chapter 46

"EEEEEEEEEEEEEEEEEEEEEEAAAAAAAA-AAAAARRRRRRRRRGGGG!"

With an ear-splitting howl, the monsters rushed to attack, claws slashing the air.

Rooted to the spot, I dug my toe claws into the floor.

"Run, Gruff," I heard Paul cry.

But I couldn't. The red eyes crackled with fire as the whole pack crouched to spring. I forced myself to wait, not moving a muscle.

And the instant Ripper gave the signal to pounce, I snatched the fire hose out of the pool and reached behind me to turn it up full blast. Then I pointed it at the airborne werewolves.

Steam hissed and sizzled as the heavy stream of water crashed into the monsters. They shrieked and howled in pain and fear, falling on each other in their rush to get away.

The ones farthest away from me threw themselves through the windows and dived out the door, racing to escape. Clouds of steam billowed into the air, filling the rec building with fog so thick I could hardly see to aim my hose.

"AIEEEEEEEEEEEEEEEEEEEEEE!," screamed

the monsters. "AAAAAAAAAAAAAAAAA-AAAIIIIIIIIII!"

They slipped in the puddles of water and fought each other in their scramble to escape the hose.

"*Let us go!*" they cried into my head. "*We won't come back!*"

"*You bet you won't,*" I snarled and moved toward them with the hose.

Werewolves gibbered and whimpered, climbing on top of their fallen friends to reach high windows and leap out. They jammed the narrow doorway lashing at each other to make space for themselves.

The ones that got out quickly leaped the fence and melted away into the woods.

Then I heard a noise that made my heart swell with wonder.

"AAAAAAAAAAAAAAAAAOOOOOOOOOO-OOOOOOOOOOO!"

Not a werewolf howl but Wolfmother! I heard an answering howl. Thornclaw, my wolf-father! And then another came from my wolf-brother Sharpfang! My wolf family, the pack that had raised me lovingly from a baby, had come to help me again!

My wolf family's attack howls were quickly joined by a hundred more wolves. They'd all come back to chase off the escaping were-wolves.

I was so thrilled I forgot the hose. In a mad dash, the last of the werewolves in the rec building scrambled for the door. As they pushed each other aside in their hurry to get out, I recognized Mr. Parker.

My heart skipped. I couldn't let him run off with the other werewolves. Quickly I brought the hose up again and aimed it at him. The stream of water fell short. I was too far away.

I ran forward and almost fell as the hose snagged on something. Another werewolf leaped over one of its injured friends and out the door. Mr. Parker was almost there. I tugged hard on the hose, grunting. It wouldn't budge. Another few seconds and Mr. Parker would be gone — he'd be a monster forever and never come back to his family.

I looked to see what was tangling the hose. It was stuck on a pipe next to the pool. I grunted in frustration. Mr. Parker had his paw on the doorjamb. There was no time to free the hose.

"I've got it Gruff!" I looked back. It was Paul, pulling the hose free.

I stumbled as the water suddenly gushed out, harder than ever. Mr. Parker was half out the door. I hit him with the full force of the hose.

The water lifted him right into the air and slammed him headfirst into the wall.

The Parker werewolf went limp and slumped to the floor.

I dropped the hose. Mr. Parker didn't move. The last of the werewolves leaped out the door and ran off into the woods. The howls of the real wolves grew fainter as they chased the monsters deeper into the boggy swamp.

I ran to Mr. Parker. His red eyes were closed.

Had I killed him instead of saving him?

Chapter 47

Moaning miserably, I leaned over the unconscious werewolf and bent my ear to his chest to listen for a heartbeat. I closed my eyes to concentrate.

A weight came down on my shoulder. I flinched and jumped three feet in the air, extending all my claws for battle. But it wasn't a werewolf, it was Paul.

He flinched away from me, then stood his ground. "You saved us, Gruff," he said in a shaky voice. "Thank you."

"Gruff?!" Kim had come up behind Paul. She stared at me in shock and disgust. "That monster can't be Gruff."

"Yes, Kim," Paul said calmly. "He saved us. And now we have to save him."

I looked at Paul in surprise.

"The people," said Paul, looking nervously over his shoulder back at the pool. People were starting to climb out as the howls of the werewolves grew fainter in the distance. "They were too scared to see what really happened. All they know is monsters tried to get them, and you look like one of the — uh — monsters.

When they get their courage back, they'll come after you."

Paul was right. Already I heard grumbling and angry shouts coming from the crowd of people climbing out of the pool.

"There's one that didn't get away," a man yelled.

"Let's get him!" shouted another.

Paul plucked at my arm. "Come on, Gruff, we'd better hurry." He looked at the limp were-wolf on the floor. "Is that a friend of yours?" he asked worriedly. "It may slow you down too much if you have to carry him."

Suddenly Kim gasped. She sank to her knees beside the injured werewolf. "Daddy!" she cried. "Daddy!"

The blood drained out of Paul's face. He stared at me. "Is it true?" he whispered hoarsely.

I nodded. Behind us the crowd of people were getting louder. Some had found a pile of lumber and were arming themselves with heavy chunks of wood. "We'll teach those creatures," they grumbled. "We'll teach them to attack our town."

Quickly I tossed Mr. Parker over my shoulder. I held out my arm. Kim hesitated a second then jumped up and clung to my shoulder. Paul leaped up beside her. The crowd roared. People screamed at me to let them go.

"It's all right!" Paul shouted. "He helped us. He won't hurt us."

But the people were shouting for blood. They couldn't hear him. I ran out the door, the crowd close on my heels.

Chapter 48

I staggered into the backyard of the Parker house and collapsed on the ground. We'd left the angry crowd of people behind but it hadn't been easy.

Paul hurried to unlock the door. The three of us carried Mr. Parker inside. "What will we do with him?" asked Kim in a trembling voice. "Will he ever be human again?"

I'd had an idea working in my head as we ran back to the house. I didn't know how dangerous it was or even if it would work, but we had to try it. I'd managed to keep the werewolf book with me through everything and now I put it on the table and again opened it to the "Rules of The Wereing."

"You know what to do?" asked Paul eagerly, stepping up to look.

I jabbed my claw at one of the rules. *"A werewolf cannot tolerate anything silver,"* it said.

"Silver," mused Kim.

"Silver?" asked Paul. "But what will that do?"

"I get it!" cried Kim. She ran to the dining room and came back with a silver tray and two

154

candlesticks. She dumped them on the floor. "You check the bedrooms, Paul. Get anything silver — picture frames, necklaces, anything!"

Kim hurried out of the room.

Mr. Parker was breathing normally now. I didn't think he would be unconscious much longer. There was no time to lose. I leaped up the stairs at one bound, going all the way to the attic. I'd seen a trunk there once when Paul was showing me around. It was full of old toys Mrs. Parker couldn't bear to throw away.

I dumped the toys out and hauled the big trunk back downstairs to the living room. What would happen if this didn't work? I'd seen the Parker werewolf try to save Kim but I'd also seen him bite another human. And in the end he had tried to escape into the woods with the werewolves.

If we couldn't cure Mr. Parker — the dad werewolf — I was afraid of what he might do to his own family when he woke up.

Chapter 49

I opened the lid of the trunk and gestured at Kim and Paul. Nodding, they dumped all the silver they could find into the trunk — knives and forks, neck chains, pitchers, candlesticks, everything.

Being near so much silver was hard for me. My muscles began to ache and cramp. Shooting pains stabbed my arms and legs. I grew too weak to lift Mr. Parker by myself.

But once I made Kim and Paul understand what we had to do, they took his legs, I took his arms and we put him into the trunk with the silver.

Instantly, the Parker werewolf came awake.

"RRRRRRRRRROOOOOOOOOOOOOOOO-OOWWWWWWWWWWWRRRRRR!"

It bellowed in shock. The werewolf grabbed the sides of the trunk to heave itself out, its eyes blazing. I grabbed the lid of the trunk and banged it down, jumping on top of it. I motioned to Kim and Paul to quick lock the trunk.

But the werewolf reared up, roaring, and bumped me off the lid. As I tumbled to the floor it hissed at Kim and Paul. Patches of its coarse gray fur flew through the air. It had one leg out of the trunk when I reached up and pushed the lid hard, sending it crashing down on the werewolf's head.

It whirled, swiping at me and baring its fangs. The sudden movement threw it off balance and as the werewolf tried to spring out of the box, it slipped on all the silver inside and fell heavily. I pounced, wrestling it back into the trunk.

Pain sapped the strength from my limbs everywhere I touched a piece of silver. Strange sour-smelling smoke rose from the Parker werewolf. It tried to push me off its chest but its muscles were weakening. I pulled myself up. Paul grabbed my shoulders and he and Kim dragged me out of the trunk.

Again I climbed on the lid. This time I collapsed on top of it, my chest heaving with the effort for breath. Kim locked the lid in place.

For a few minutes everything was quiet and still. Then the werewolf inside started howling and banging on the inside of the lid. Its cries of pain were horrible.

"It hurts!" Mr. Parker screamed into my aching head. *"Let me out. You're killing me."*

Paul and Kim couldn't understand what it was saying but I agonized. Should I let it out? Would the silver kill it?

Then the pitiful cries changed to roars of rage. The lid bulged from the efforts of the werewolf inside. It screamed and howled and banged.

CRACK!

The lid wasn't going to hold. Kim and Paul, their eyes wide and blank with pain, jumped up on the lid to help me hold it down. They sat on either side of me, gripping each other's hands and grasping tight onto my coarse fur.

After a long time, the bangs and howls grew weaker. And weaker. Until at last there was no movement at all from inside the trunk.

Kim and Paul looked at each other and at me, their eyes big and fearful. Had I killed their dad? Or was the werewolf just biding its time, waiting?

There was only one way to find out. Kim and Paul climbed down. Kim unlocked the trunk.

Carefully, I lifted the lid.

Chapter 50

Mr. Parker, human and shivering, lay inside, half covered with dented, twisted, and blackened silver. He blinked up at us, then looked in wonder at his smooth tanned arms.

"I'm myself again," he whispered. "I'm human."

"He's freezing," said Kim, grabbing a blanket from a basket by the stairs. She tucked it around her father and hugged his neck. "Oh, Daddy, we were so scared. Are you really back to normal?"

Mr. Parker shuddered and pulled the blanket tighter around him. "Yes," he said in a stronger voice. "It's over."

I stepped back and Paul and Kim helped him out of the trunk. "It all seems like a nightmare," he said, slumping into a chair. Then he frowned at me. "But it was no dream, was it?"

I shook my shaggy head slowly.

The front door flew open with a bang. Mr. Parker jumped to his feet, reaching for Kim and Paul. I flattened myself against the wall, ready to spring.

"Oh!" cried Mrs. Parker, sagging breathlessly against the door. "You're all right! Thank heavens! I ran all the way here. I heard the monsters had got you. But — "

She suddenly broke off with a scream. Mrs. Parker had caught sight of me. She shrank away in horror.

Paul ran to her. "Mom, it's okay. He's not really a monster. He's Gruff. He helped us. He saved the whole town from the werewolves. He saved Dad, too. Dad was a werewolf but Gruff turned him back into a person."

But Mrs. Parker didn't seem to hear. Her eyes were fixed on me and her hand was feeling behind her for a weapon, any weapon.

"Look, Mommy, I'll prove it," cried Kim. She rushed over to me and threw her arms around me, looking up into my hideous monster face. "You're our brother, Gruff, and we love you. No matter what."

My stomach twisted and a fist squeezed my heart. My throat started to close up and my eyes burned. Something was terribly wrong.

I was crying. Painful werewolf tears that burned my snout.

Chapter 51

Mrs. Parker, it seemed, had missed everything. The last thing she remembered was seeing some hideous creature come flying out of a tree straight at her. She had been knocked unconscious and only woke a little while ago, covered with a plastic tablecloth and hidden under a picnic table.

It must have been Mr. Parker who did that, I thought, slipping out the back door while Kim and Paul and Mr. Parker tried to fill Mrs. Parker in on all that had happened.

I stood under the silvery moon, feeling good that my new family was safe from the night creatures.

I lifted my snout into the clean-smelling air and howled. "AAAAAAAAAAAAAAOOOOO-OOOOOOOOOO!"

The howl stirred my blood in a sad way. The wind ruffled my fur.

"AAAAAAAAAAAOOOOOOOOOOOOOOOO-OOOOOOOO!"

My ears pricked up. An answering howl! Wolfmother! Then I heard the howls of Thornclaw and Sharpfang, my wolffather and wolfbrother, joining in.

Their howls came from far, far away. They were saying good-bye.

And this time, I knew, that strong, sad howling meant good-bye forever. They knew I was one of the humans now and I would stay with the humans.

Now that I knew the "Rules of The Wereing" I could keep my town safe from werewolves. If I wanted to, I could even kill the monster within me and be human myself from now on.

But I still had work to do. Tomorrow night, before the moon rose, Rick would go into the trunk, if he was still around. And then any other humans that had been bitten by werewolves but hadn't run away would also go into the trunk and be cured. But not me.

The werewolves were gone. They might not be back next month or even next year, but someday they would return. Something about Fox Hollow drew them here. But when they came I'd be ready for them.

And I would need my werewolf powers to defeat them. There was no escape from my fate.

"I am a monster!" I howled.

A good monster. And I have to stay that way.

About the Authors

RODMAN PHILBRICK and LYNN HARNETT are the authors of another popular Apple Paperback series, The House on Cherry Street. Rodman Philbrick has written numerous mysteries and suspense stories for adults, and the much acclaimed young adult novels *Freak the Mighty* and *The Fire Pony*. Lynn Harnett is an award-winning journalist and a founding editor of *Kidwriters Monthly*. The husband-and-wife writing team divide their time between Kittery, Maine, and the Florida Keys.